HAUNTED WITCH

A SEASHELL COVE PARANORMAL MYSTERY

T. THORN COYLE

For my Kickstarter supporters.
May one thousand blessings rain upon your life.

Welcome to Seashell Cove, where the waves are treacherous, and the inhabitants are... strange.

1

———

It was a beautiful spring day in Seashell Cove, which meant light rain with intermittent sun, and a temperature of sixty-five degrees Fahrenheit. My spirits were up, and breakfast with my boyfriend, Stefon, had only improved things.

The bookstore was fairly busy, even for a Sunday afternoon. About six people browsed the stacks or were tucked into reading chairs scattered here and there beneath windows or in lamplit corners.

The Widening Gyre is the reason I returned to Seashell Cove after going to college up in Portland. It's the family shop, and with both of my parents gone now, the tiny palace of books is all mine. Well, mine and Rhiannon's, the black cat currently blinking green eyes at me from the long wood countertop.

Well...mine, Rhiannon's, and Biff the ghost's. Biff has been here longer than any of us, and owned the shop when he was alive. He died when I was a little kid, and the photos he took of Seashell Cove from the 1960s through the 1990s still hung on the walls in between the wooden bookshelves he'd made by hand back in the day.

The bookshelves had been gleaming in the sun for the past half hour. The golden sheen also graced the current indie author bestsellers display on the bookshelves closest to the door, lighting up the bright covers.

Hopefully it would help sell a few.

My name is Sarah Endora Braxton—name a deliberate misspelling of the Stevie Nicks song—and the less we say about my middle name, the better. The only person who uses it is my honorary uncle, Cyrus, and then only when he's feeling particularly exasperated. Luckily, strange and magical Seashell Cove had been quiet since the winter excitement and I'd been determined to settle into my witch studies, so Uncle Cyrus was currently pretty happy with me.

All in all, life was good. Add in a little sunshine and a cup of tea? I was one happy Sarah.

On spring days like this one, I could barely contain a hum of contentment. Smiling, I reached for my fourth mug of tea for the day as Rhiannon cocked her head and sneezed.

Onto my hand.

Into my mug.

Oh well, the tea needed refreshing, anyway.

"Thanks a lot, Rhiannon," I said, reaching for a tissue from the box beneath the counter to wipe my fingers.

She just licked her whiskers and ignored me, turning her whole body to face the front of the shop, as if trying to decide if a spot of window sun was in her immediate future. I couldn't blame her.

May in our quirky little town on the Oregon coast is a sweet time. With the intermittent sun and light rain blessing the earth, the gnomes and other fae spirits in charge of gardens were all lively and happy. The chaneques—Mexican fae beings—were working hard in the garden of the Vargas's tamale shop next door. I could hear the digging of their little shovels and their small boots stomping about.

It was also a good time for all the shops on Main Street, because folks were out and about again. Not only were the locals happy with the weather, which increased foot traffic, but the early tourists had begun to arrive.

After the events of January, I needed a sweet time. I had finally recovered from the murder of the dryad and was past the phase of testing and ordeals at the hands of whatever super-secret witchy-warlock counsel Uncle Cyrus was part of. Turns out, every witch or warlock went through that around age twenty-eight.

My testing turned out to be less than ordinary in that they sent someone with a vendetta against my parents who really, really wanted to kill me for some reason.

But, you know, water under the bridge. Right?

Oh, added to that was taking up the mantle of Justice left by my parents, which was not a job I'd ever wanted. I had watched it take its toll on my dad, and plus, it turned out that work had been partially to blame for my mother's death. Cyrus couldn't prove it, but it seemed pretty clear.

But...the powers that be had decided I had avoided my destiny long enough.

Some people, it turns out, can dodge their destinies for quite some time. Not witches. Once you reached a certain age—in my case, the tolling bell of my first Saturn Return at, you guessed it, age twenty-eight—time was simply up. Around that time, a person had to face down their destiny and decide who was in charge. Otherwise, things tended to not go very well.

Believe me, I decided pretty quickly that me being in charge of my own destiny was a much better deal than the other way around.

So here I was, proprietor of The Widening Gyre, New and Used Books and Fancies. I was also a hereditary witch, and what passed for a magical detective around these parts.

At least I had help with that. My uncle Cyrus had semi-permanently moved back to the area. Well, Portland, which was closer to Seashell Cove than Paris. And I was settling into my routine, trying to make the bookstore a success, and spending more time with Stefon than I used to. I finally realized how much I'd grown to count on him for support. Not only was he tall, dark, and handsome, he was also quite literally my knight in shining armor. He'd stood at my side during the magical battle to take down the sorcerer responsible for the death of the dryad and my mother, despite not having any magic himself.

It didn't take long after that to give in to what had been building between us.

And by give in, I mean tell that handsome knight that I loved him. Let's just say that Valentine's Day was extra-special. Like, dancing-unicorn-and-glittery-twenty-sided-dice special.

But as I said, on the magic front, things had been blessedly quiet. That gave me a chance to practice my witchy skills in a more leisurely fashion. And to focus on the bookstore, which, despite the day's customers, still needed some help.

"But we're doing a little bit better, aren't we, Rhiannon?"

The shop cat didn't deign to reply. With bright green eyes and a mind of her own, Rhiannon could run the place if she wasn't so lazy. She yawned at me from her perch on the desktop where I was packaging up shipments to head out with the parcel service. Speaking of which, I really need to finish it up. The driver would be arriving soon.

I heard a gasp, and a whispered "Stop it! Be serious!" from the back of the store. Tracy and Tabitha were doing their usual Sunday afternoon browse in the paranormal/occult section. They were two teenagers I met on their winter break from school, and once they found out that not only was I a witch, but that the bookstore had its own ghost, they'd been haunting the stacks every week.

So far, all Biff had done was throw a couple of books on the floor when the teens were around, but that seemed to be enough for them. It didn't take much to keep spooky teenagers happy, and I knew that firsthand.

I had been one myself.

If I'd stayed in Portland, I might've even maintained more of my Goth sensibilities, but in a sleepy town like

Seashell Cove? Where you need to wear fleece and sensible boots for the bulk of the year? Pretty much everyone just succumbed to what I called "Basic Pacific Northwest," which was a uniform of jeans, sweaters, and heavy rain jackets in shades that ranged from forest green to navy to burgundy for the more daring. Oh, and either rain or rugged hiking boots for the practical, though the hiking boots are special-ordered in black if you're a person like myself.

I weighed and stamped the final package, and stacked up the orders in neat piles at the end of the counter, ready and waiting for the parcel pick-up truck.

The shop door slammed opened, sending the bells clanging. Rhiannon hissed, tail swishing at the disturbance.

In burst the newest resident of Seashell Cove, tan trench coat fluttering around his too-big jeans and battered sneakers. Chip Lancaster, camera phone aloft, had a very determined look on his face.

It was a look I'd unfortunately grown used to. I did not like it one bit.

"Sarah Braxton! The citizens of Seashell Cove demand answers!"

2

———

I bit back a startled growl.

"You have got to be kidding me."

Chip swooped close enough for me to see the bleeding corners of his fingernails where he must have been biting hangnails. I danced and dodged behind the counter, trying to avoid that dang camera phone.

Chip Lancaster was a self-styled independent journalist and blogger or VideoTube-er, or TokTok-er, or whatever the heck people were using these days. I avoided social media like the plague, much to the dismay of the teenagers who really wanted me to "put the store on the map" and rolled their eyes when I objected, accusing me of being old.

Considering my actual age, I had to admit, that stung.

Chip had barged in a month back, insisting the public had a right to know about Biff.

I had sweetly asked him to leave. He wouldn't.

Luckily, my very large boyfriend happened to have been on site and kindly showed him to the door.

But today, it was just me, and the still-browsing customers who hadn't yet been alerted to the disturbance in the air.

"Sarah Braxton, do you have any comments?"

I held up my right hand.

My casting hand.

"Stop right there, Chip. And put down your camera. I already told you I don't know a person named Biff."

The fact that I knew a *ghost* named Biff was beside the point. I mean, some people would argue that ghosts still have personhood, yada yada, but I wasn't going to split those hairs. The ghost was a ghost, and if saying I didn't know any people named Biff kept Chip out of the bookstore, my small prevarication was fine with me.

He leaned even closer, looming across the counter despite my protestation, still waving the camera phone around in a menacing fashion.

Chip was one of those early-twenty-something white kids who—in a place that wasn't Seashell Cove— would've been a barista, or a skateboarder, or something more useful to society than whatever he was.

I mean, I have a lot of friends who went to art school—my ex-girlfriend Cecilia among them—and I'm not one to squash other people's dreams. I even think that journalism is still important, indie journalism included. Folks who put themselves out there to cover right wing protests at the state capitol? I had nothing but respect for their efforts.

But that wasn't Chip.

With his sandy, unkempt hair and pasty skin, face slightly bloated from copious amounts of salt and sugar, Chip was one of those basement-dwelling annoyances that I wasn't predisposed to think too kindly of. He was some weird cross between a self-styled journalist and one of those old-fashioned paranormal investigator type cranks that used to have late night radio shows back when I was still a kid.

Come to think of it, those cranks should have swarmed Seashell Cove and never did. I would have to ask Uncle Cyrus about that. I bet my parents had something to do with maintaining a bubble of protection around Seashell Cove. I mean, people came for the super-haunted Historic Kelpie Inn up the highway, but that was sold as all in good fun, kind of like the McMinnville UFO Festival.

It wasn't supposed to be serious.

The fact that Chip's seriously obnoxious self got through meant those protections must be fraying.

I gave an internal sigh and added "reinforce Seashell Cove wards" to my growing list of tasks. Though how one went about protecting a whole town, I had not a clue.

"This isn't about Biff," Chip sputtered, eyes gleaming dangerously, "though I still think you're lying about the ghost. Everyone knows your shop is haunted."

Once again, I tried to dodge the camera, but he just kept coming. Rhiannon arched her back and hissed again, giving the camera a swipe before leaping from the counter to barrel towards the back of the shop.

Chip yelped and stuck his stuck a finger in his mouth.

"Your cat drew blood," he said. "If I get some strange disease, you're paying for it."

A few customers poked their heads out from between the stacks, trying to figure out what the commotion was about. I heard the pitter-patter of sneakered feet, and sure enough, here came the teenagers.

Tabitha and Tracy.

"Do you need help?" Tabitha asked, hands on her hips. An Asian teen with dark hair cut into a bob, today she wore maroon boots, dark gray jeans, and a long maroon sweater topped with a striped scarf. Her best friend and counterpart, Tracy, was a blond, peaches-and-cream white girl also in jeans, but hers were black, and her oversized sweater was a pale blue that matched her eyes.

Her witch of a mother had the same blond hair and blue eyes.

And by witch of a mother, I mean, it turned out Tracy's mother, Carol, was actually a witch like me.

I found that out when we faced down the sorcerer who everyone thought had just been sent to test me, and she had. But she also came to Seashell Cove with another agenda and was currently serving time planting three thousand trees to recompense for the killing of a dryad.

"I don't need any help, but thanks," I replied. "Chip here was just leaving."

"I am not! I demand to know. My public demands..."

Tabitha stepped forward, Tracy right behind her, arms crossed over their chests.

"You're making an awful lot of demands, mister," Tracy said.

Chip paused and puffed up his chest. "That's because I'm a *journalist*. And as a journalist I have a right to know what's happening in Seashell Cove."

"So what is happening?" Tabitha asked.

"There's been a murder at The Kelpie Inn." He turned to me and pointed. "And I think you know all about it."

"Human, fae, or something else?"

It was a question I had to ask, because you just never knew in Seashell Cove. There were some seriously weird beings living in and around the town.

"Human," he spat out, phone still waving in the air.

I'd had enough of that. "Can I see your phone?" I held out my hand.

"What? No!"

He feinted toward me, and then jerked away, just as Tabitha and Tracy flanked him. Tracy bumped his hip as Tabitha reached in and grabbed for the shiny object.

Chip yelped and fumbled the slippery phone, sending it skittering across the hardwood floor.

I dove around the counter, hand reaching for the phone just as his reached, too. Our foreheads smacked in some weird slapstick moment, just as the magic in my right hand loosed itself and zapped his still-filming phone.

The scent of fried electronics joined the smell of books, lemon wood polish, and tea.

"You broke my phone!"

I hadn't intended on it, but clearly my subconscious felt otherwise. I gave an internal shrug.

Sometimes a witch has to do what a witch has to do.

"Cool!" Tabitha exclaimed. "Did you see that?" She turned to Tracy. The other teen stood very still, mouth hanging open as if she had just seen some amazing feat.

Well, I guess she had, but after the big battle they witnessed when we took down the sorcerer, me zapping someone's phone hardly seemed like cause for excitement.

"Don't think I'll ever get used to that," Tracy murmured.

"That makes two of us," I replied. I studiously ignored the other customers who seemed split between standing slack-jawed like Tracy or pretending that nothing strange had just happened.

Uncle Cyrus would not be pleased. My using magic inadvertently like that was a problem. And using it in front of civilians? Even worse.

But that was a problem for another day. Right now, I had to deal with a sputtering Chip Lancaster.

"I can't believe you broke my phone!" the intrepid citizen reporter moaned, scrambling on the floor as if picking up bits of shattered electronics.

Picking up pieces of his dignity, more like, because other than a slight crack in the screen I couldn't see anything else wrong with the device, though he cradled it as if it were a wounded bird.

He glared at me. "You owe me a phone."

"I don't know what you're talking about. You're the one who barged in here, pointing that thing in my face when I asked you not to. And I didn't drop the thing."

No need to mention that little zap. Maybe the people who'd seen the magic would think they'd imagined the spark that shorted out Chip's electronics.

One could hope.

Chip drew himself up in his trench coat, chin thrust into the air like Napoleon. "I told you, I am a journalist."

"I don't think so," Tracy muttered.

He whirled to glare at her. "Who are you?"

"Okay. Stop," I said, before he could get into it with the teens. "Everybody calm down."

I snapped my fingers. "Chip."

He looked at me, eyes startled. Did I see a flash of fear?

"What do you know?" I asked him.

Whatever I'd seen in his eyes fled and he was all belligerent arrogance again. He smirked and crossed his arms over his chest. "Maybe if you buy me a new phone, I'll tell you. Though as a journalist I don't owe you anything."

I stepped back around the counter and slammed open the cash register drawer. Most people pay with a card these days, but I keep some cash on hand just in case. Though I must say, I never expected that paying off a citizen journalist would be one of my petty cash expenses. I counted out five twenties and held the small fan of bills across the counter.

Chip looked from the money, to me, and back to the money.

"One hundred bucks? This was a top of the line..."

"It's either this or nothing," I replied, still holding out the cash. "Do you want it or not?"

With two strides forward, he reached out and ripped the money from my hand.

"Okay!" Tracy said, "Spill."

3

My shop assistant, Duncan, had loped in for his shift not long after the phone debacle.

A nerdy white guy with black-framed glasses, Duncan wore skater sneakers and had a burgeoning belly that smoothed out his Octavia Butler T-shirt. He was able to take care of the remaining customers at the front desk as the teens and I grilled Chip Lancaster in one of the seating nooks near the back of the store, trying to get to the bottom of what the heck he was even talking about.

Along with copious amounts of my best Darjeeling, getting the story out of the guy required much massaging of his ego. Finally, I gave up and called The Historic Kelpie to see what I could find out myself.

No one answered, which wasn't good. I did not leave a voicemail.

What would I even say? "Excuse me, but did someone get murdered at your historic inn?" Friendly as I was with Liam, the owner, a person just did not leave that sort of a message.

Ever.

After that, I convinced Chip it was in his best interests to leave by mentioning the safety of any future phones he might acquire.

So? I can't be nice all the time.

As a result, the teens and I were headed up the highway in my little bright orange electric Fiat. I had to fold my Amazonian frame into the car, but it was well worth it. The sun shone on the ocean and a phalanx of bright kites hovered above the cliffs, long tails flapping in the ocean wind. There was a dragon, an orca, two elaborate box kites, and a few diamond shapes dyed with fantastic colors.

The view was quintessential Seashell Cove.

Yeah, this was definitely my favorite time of year.

The teens gabbled excitedly in the backseat as I drove. I swear, they made me feel so old. But though I rolled my eyes at their antics sometimes, they were actually quite steady. And they'd been a big help, too.

We might even be heading into friendship territory, if two teenagers and a twenty-eight-year-old nerd could ever really be friends.

It had been far too long since I'd visited The Historic Kelpie.

It was Seashell Cove's most famous spot, and a favorite with tourists, which was a good thing, it being an inn and all. Oh, some people preferred the more upscale beachside hotel just up the highway, but if you wanted quirky? The Historic Kelpie was your place.

The inn was notoriously haunted, which was part

of its attraction. The teenagers insisted this would be a good marketing ploy for my bookshop, too. They rightfully said that people from all over would come by to take their picture with Biff the ghost if only I would let them "manage my social media presence."

First of all, how do you take a picture with a ghost?

Second, a bunch of looky-loos was exactly what I was afraid of. There was just no guarantee that any of those people would buy a darn thing. At least you had to book a room at The Historic Kelpie to risk a ghostly encounter. The door of The Widening Gyre was open to anyone who wandered by on Main Street.

I buzzed my window down, and the ocean air rushed into the car. "Too windy back there?" I asked the teens.

"We're fine," Tabitha replied.

"Smells great," Tracy said.

It did smell good. There was nothing like the breeze of the Pacific. I smiled at the two faces in my rearview mirror. The blond-haired, cherub-cheeked Tracy, and the raven-haired Tabitha who was going to be a real looker when she was a few years older.

Luckily, both teens were smart. I just hoped they were smart enough to navigate being attractive young women in a world that seemed to want to eat young people alive.

A rush of affection filled me as I returned my eyes to the road, and the cars chugging in both directions past the outlet mall and the beachside parking lots.

Little by little, the teens were wearing me down on the ghost thing. Turns out they knew more about marketing than I did, go figure. Considering I'd spent several years juggling the limping store finances while taking care of my dying father, I'd left the dubious joys of online interaction far behind.

Up on the left was a big, professionally carved wood sign. A black horse with a flowing mane galloped over waves, hooves leaping above a giant red kraken that reached its sinuous arms up to grasp the curving letters that spelled out *The Historic Kelpie Inn*.

I waited for a rumbling delivery truck to pass before turning left across the highway, which was always a hair-raising proposition. I made it safely across and pulled into the tiny front parking lot of The Kelpie. Half a block down was a larger guest parking lot that skirted the back of the inn, but it was a pain to get into, and if you didn't have luggage to unload, wasn't worth risking the traffic.

The three slots out front butted against a six-foot-tall painted turquoise fence festooned with whales, and fish, and mermaids. A starfish held a maraca in one curled arm as a purple squid played trumpet.

Like I said, quirky.

I'd always loved The Historic Kelpie. When I was around the teens' age, Cecilia and I hung out with our friends in the garden-woods-art installation warren behind the guest parking lot and the main building of the inn.

The inn compound was composed of two long, low 1950s outbuildings that were kitted out into separate family suites with two or three bedrooms, pocket kitchens, and "living rooms" with fake electric fireplaces, old, overstuffed furniture, and more outlandish art.

Through the courtyard and past the painted gates stood an old three-story building with a broad front porch. It must've been over a hundred years old, hence the ghosts.

Tracy tugged on the gate and turned.

"It's locked," she said. "What now?"

The gate shouldn't be locked. It never was, during the day. My witch's intuition pinged, but I shrugged it off. It was probably just closed because of this alleged murder Chip Livingston was on about.

That was the logical explanation.

Right?

4

I must have been staring at the aquamarine wall for awhile, because Tabitha cleared her throat and repeated Tracy's question. "Sarah? What now?"

I pasted a fake smile on my face.

"Guess we'll walk around the back," I said. "We can get to the main door that way."

The teens exchanged a look, but said nothing.

We headed to the sidewalk and walked the few yards down to the steep gravel parking lot with its sharp turn off the highway. The parking lot was pleasant once it finally evened out, being sheltered by towering firs and pines. Only a couple of cars were parked though, which was strange, given the season.

Maybe there really had been a murder.

Our boots crunched up the gravel and I inhaled the scent of ocean and Douglas fir. That was the scent of the Oregon coast, right there. It was my favorite perfume.

I liked it even better than Uncle Cyrus's combination of Bay Rum and frankincense.

They only scent I liked better was the smell of my boyfriend Stefon's, skin. That scent made me want to lick things.

Boyfriend. I turned that word over in my mind because it was still new. After our trial by fire in January, I'd decided he was worth risking my heart for.

He hadn't proved me wrong yet.

We passed whimsical sculptures of crabs, seashells, more mermaids, and a diver in an old-fashioned bell helmet, and headed back through the side to the garden courtyard at the center of all the buildings.

I thumped up onto the big front porch of the main building and patted the porch shark on its nose.

The thing about that shark? Not only was it eight feet long, it had a saddle like a horse, making it a very popular photo op for the tourists. The shark was almost as popular as the ghosts themselves.

I tugged on the right side of the carved wood doors with matching stained glass windows. They were heavy enough that I had to put a little muscle into it to open the thing all the way.

We stepped in to the mingled fragrances of popcorn and dust.

The popcorn scent came from the old-fashioned movie theater popcorn machine to my right, and the dust? I was never sure if that was from the old 1930s overstuffed furniture, or the ghosts.

"Where do you think we should go?" Tabitha asked, after we'd wiped our boots on the broad mat that covered a few square feet of hideous Art Deco–era lobby carpeting. "I don't see anybody."

I shrugged and looked around at the old movie posters, Deco floor lamps, and a low shelf filled with handmade soaps and postcards depicting the inn and Seashell Cove itself. A bookshelf next to it was filled with a lending library from local authors and writers who had stayed at the inn.

"Hello!" Tracy called out.

We heard voices murmuring in the back, past the little lobby area.

We wound our way off the carpet and onto hardwood floors, stepping into an old, cavernous bar lit with red and amber lights. Artwork covered every surface, and there was a beaded curtain to the right for those who wanted the one private booth. A long wood bar was hung with fishing floats and nets, and an old, mottled mirror reflected half empty bottles and gleaming glassware.

A jukebox hunched in one corner, near an open door that I knew led to the big communal dining area and kitchen.

The voices were coming from back there somewhere. I took the lead and walked on through from the low-ceilinged, cozy bar to the much more spacious, wood-timbered space of the dining room. It still wasn't a huge space. There was one long communal table in the center, surrounded by mismatched chairs. Six wooden booths lined the edges, and multipaned windows let in spring sunshine and the shadowy green of the garden outside.

The teens talked softly with each other, pointing to

things on the walls as we walked. And given that the walls were pretty much covered with art, sculptures, and trinkets, and that a rowboat and manta ray hung from the ceiling, there was a lot to look at. And that was before the wooden phone box, and the needlepoint cushions depicting giant sea creatures eating boats.

I looked over my shoulder. "Haven't you been here before?"

Both teens shook their heads.

"Not inside," Tracy said.

"It's really amazing, isn't it?"

They both nodded, and continued to stare.

Sure enough, the voices were coming from the kitchen. I knocked on the wooden swinging door, then pushed my way through, entering what was once a small restaurant kitchen, and was now a communal place for people staying at the inn who wanted to cook their own meals. Liam is a bit of an eccentric hippie that way.

But what can I say? It worked for the historic inn, and the patrons who loved it, really loved it. The ones who were expecting fancy televisions and bland rooms with corporate art and big, ordinary looking beds, and an ironing board in an ample closet? They were always disappointed and never came back.

Liam said he didn't need that kind of trade. He ran the inn the way he wanted to, and the people that wanted what he liked? They were the only customers he cared to cater to.

Besides, he got most of his money from ghost hunters, and they were eccentric, too. So it worked.

Liam himself was slumped over one of the scarred

and battered butcher block counters, and next to the white porcelain sink under a window looking out onto The Kelpie's back garden was Delta Crabbit, white hair pulled back in an untidy bun, tanned and weathered face looking grim. I knew she was friends with Liam, but for some reason, I hadn't expected to see the witch there.

"Sarah," she said, by way of greeting.

I stopped inside the door near the bank of four microwave ovens that crouched—smeared with finger-prints—on a metal shelving unit that also held assorted cookware and mixing bowls. People swore one of the microwaves was haunted, though they never seemed to agree on which one, or what exactly tipped them off.

The smart ones used the microwave and coffee maker provided in each room, and never ventured into the kitchen. But the hard-core ghosties? Apparently loved risking their frozen burritos getting haunted from a random microwave zap.

That was The Kelpie for you. And really, that was just Seashell Cove. Everything in town was slightly askew, though it was often hard to pinpoint exactly what was off.

Liam looked up, his white skin blotchy, and his usually clear brown eyes shot through with red, as if he'd been rubbing them. Or crying.

"You know," Liam said, voice flat. "How? Who told you?"

I took a step toward one leg of the butcher block ell. Tabitha and Tracy moved with me, standing so close that Tracy bumped my foot. I glared, and both teens jumped, but backed up a little, back toward the swinging door.

"Our intrepid citizen journalist burst into the bookstore shouting that someone had been murdered and I knew something."

"Knew something?" Liam tugged at his already disheveled brown hair and lurched toward the giant white refrigerator in the corner. The appliance had to be as old as I was, and probably sucked up more electricity than was decent. It made me wonder how high The Kelpie's electric bill was.

He bent and started clinking glass inside the fridge. Old, worn blue jeans hung from his skinny butt, just below a white and red strip of underpants elastic. Liam didn't care much for fashion, and spent all of his money running the historic inn, and collecting treasures that other people would call trash.

Finally, he emerged with a dark green bottle of beer. Lifting the bottle, he raised an eyebrow in question.

Everyone in the room shook their heads. Liam closed the fridge door with a heavy thunk, and levered the bottle against an opener nailed to the side of one of the yellow kitchen cabinets. The cap snicked off and bounced on the counter, stopping half an inch from the edge.

He took a long swallow, Adam's apple bobbing, then wiped his mouth with the back of his hand.

"You might as well come look," he said.

Still carrying the bottle, he yanked open the garden door and led the way outside.

5
____

The space tucked behind The Historic Kelpie was a bizarre, twisted wonderland. It was half woods and half sculpture garden. Seven gold, red, and black chickens scratched and pecked in a large penned area immediately behind the sprawling old building. The coop was painted with fading yellow and red stripes and the whole chicken run had been decorated to look like some sort of poultry carnival. Weathered signs advertised various chicken sideshows and the times in which the chickens were supposedly performing feats of strength and derring-do.

Strange sculptures dotted the winding pathways that skirted vegetable and flower beds, and tall trees waved overhead. There were occasional nooks with benches where people could sit when the weather was fine and dry.

Days like today, there should have been at least one or two visitors, but the back garden was empty save for us.

Like the mostly empty parking lot, it was probably because of the murder.

"Where did it happen?" I asked Liam. "And *what* exactly happened?"

Liam was quiet, as if thinking, then jerked his head in the direction of one of the pathways, took another swig of beer, and started walking.

We all followed him like imprinted baby ducks.

The closer we got to wherever it was we were going, the more my shoulders began to hunch up around my ears. More of my witch's intuition. I exhaled slowly, and forced them back down to where they belonged.

Tabitha and Tracy were silent behind me, not even remarking on the large shark's head that burst from the earth, snapping at a real boat captained by a mannequin dressed in an old-fashioned sailor suit.

Sure enough, when we stopped at the base of a large cypress tree, my hackles were definitely up. The whole area felt bad. Wrong. But other than some churned up earth, I couldn't pinpoint why.

"We found her here," Liam said, grimacing. "Or, another guest did."

"Who was she?" I asked, gazing up at the tree, then tracing the line of its trunk back down to the spreading root base. There was a slight depression there, as if a body had nestled against the tree, with the fallen bark and fans of cypress needles crushed from the weight of it.

"An opera singer," Liam said. "Professor from the university up in Corvallis, here to do some recording at Siren Studios."

Siren was run by an old high school buddy of mine.

Well, Abe was better friends with my ex-girlfriend, Cecilia, but we still hung out for the occasional micro-brew and a friendly game of pool.

What a thing to have happen. To be an artist, come to the seaside to work on a new project, and end up dead.

Tracy wandered farther down the path, to where it curved around some low bushes before beginning an ascent up toward a side road. She looked back, blue eyes wide. For a moment, with the blond hair puffing out around her pale, white face, she looked like a star-tled Renaissance angel.

"What did you find?" I asked, heading towards her.

"What's that?" she asked, pointing at a glossy bush. The slight tremor in her voice made me think she knew exactly whatever it was.

I drew up next to her and looked down. Well, damn. I saw it too.

Tangled in the glossy, round green leaves of a jade plant, something shimmered. Something that was not made of metal or plastic.

The crumpled, gleaming object had once been a living thing.

"It's a pixie," I said. "And I think it's dead."

Actually, I knew it was dead. The flow of magic that would have signaled the spark of life was gone.

"Oh no." Liam groaned. "Could this situation get any worse?"

"Can someone get me a cloth?" I asked. "Or a small box? Or both?"

I wasn't sure what the other pixies and sprites would want to do to honor their fallen friend, but I knew we couldn't just leave it in this bush for an animal to eat. I was amazed it had lasted this long without being discovered.

Liam swallowed hard, and looked as if he were about to be sick. Then he nodded my way, and raced off, back toward the kitchen door.

Delta Crabbit slipped forward. She'd been so quiet this whole time, I'd almost forgotten the older witch was there.

Delta held out her left hand over the dead pixie, fingers splayed. They hovered over the sad, shimmering body, twitching slightly, as if she felt something.

And she probably did. I realized I had no idea what Delta's talents were, having only recently discovered she was a witch at all. She'd helped me out a lot when my would-be-assigned-tester turned murderous. We weren't exactly friends now, but had a cordial working relationship. Especially when her sidekick, Preston the crankypants gnome, wasn't around.

Heck, who was I kidding? I barely even knew what my own talents were, having avoided them for years. Oh and now look at me, acting as if I was some sort of magical detective who knew what the heck I was supposed to be doing.

Speaking of which, Tabitha and Tracy both looked at me as if waiting for me to say something profound.

"Are you picking up on anything?" I asked Delta.

The witch shook her head, face sad.

"Just traces of the sprite. The rest of it is muddled." She speared me with her watery brown eyes. "You try."

I sighed. There was no getting around it: between the teens and Delta, I had to make an attempt.

I stepped closer to the bush. "What do I do?" I asked Delta.

She shook her head, but didn't say anything, so I could tell what she was thinking, *With parents like yours, and your uncle? How in the world do you not know what to do?*

Then she *tsked*, scowled, and threw up her hands.

"Center yourself. And just see what you can sense. Sometimes it helps if you rub your hands and fingertips against each other. To wake them up, like."

I did that, rubbing my hands together as if to warm them up. I noticed both teens trying the same thing. Well, that was good. Maybe my lessons could become their lessons, even though I didn't think either of them had expressed any hidden witchy abilities as of yet. But considering that Carol, Tracy's mother, was a witch, it was probably only a matter of time.

"That's enough," Delta barked. The teens and I both snapped our hands apart, exchanging a glance.

"Right," I said, and held out my left hand, floating it tentatively about six inches above the bush. After a moment, I held out my right hand, too, then, slowly, I moved them closer to the jade plant.

Sucking in a breath, I let my fingertips hover over the crumpled form of the dead pixie. My heart lurched. The poor thing. I was sure it had done nothing to deserve such a fate.

Oh, the life of a pixie wasn't easy. There were all sorts of predators around, just waiting to take the small, bright, winged creatures out.

Mostly cats and coyotes.

But this? This had been magic, I was certain of it.

Not only was the pixie's body not mangled at all, the way it would have been had an animal been at it. But...

Its magical essence had been drained.

"I can barely feel it at all."

Delta nodded. "Anything else?"

There was something, some other kind of magic, hovering around the edges of the glossy plant.

"I'm not sure, but it feels like a bear, maybe? Something big.... But we don't have any bears here." I paused, opening my magical senses, trying to feel. "And there's something else, too."

"Centaur," Tracy said. I guess she did have powers.

I went to stand over next to a Douglas fir tree where the teens were and held up my hands again.

Delta sniffed the air. "It does smell a bit horsey."

"Why do you think it's a centaur?" I asked Tracy.

"Hold your hand right here," she said, moving her own out of the way.

I held my left hand up, replacing her hand, about six inches from the trunk of the large fir tree. Sure enough, I felt something there. It felt like magic.

And I did smell the horse scent, now.

I looked at Tracy. She looked older all of a sudden. More certain.

"I smell horse and I feel magic, but what makes you think it's centaur?"

The teen rolled her eyes at me. Not so much older, after all. "What does magic plus horse mean?"

I shook my head in annoyance. "I know that. But how do you know someone magical didn't ride a horse in here?"

Tracy shrugged. "I just know. The way you know anything."

As we talked, Tabitha had wandered down the pathway and stopped at a bench beneath one of the three apple trees in the garden. Apples liked the cold, and The Kelpie's garden's apples were the best.

"I think there's something here, too," she said. Tracy trotted toward her friend as Delta and I followed more slowly behind.

The chickens clucked from their enclosure and I could hear gulls shrieking from the beach, just down the hill. For a moment, I wished it was just an ordinary spring day. A day I could enjoy. But there was nothing ordinary about this situation.

Tracy pointed down to the softened earth. Sure enough, there were prints as if a horse had been there. But I noticed they weren't as deep as they would've been had it been a horse and a rider.

"Looks like you were right, Tracy. Centaur."

I turned to Delta. "But why would a centaur kill a pixie?"

Delta scowled. "Not for any reason I can imagine. I just know it can't be anything good."

I said nothing, but I had to agree.

6

I sat, feet curled up beneath me, ensconced on Stefon's comfy leather sofa. The gas fireplace was lit, and the view out the floor-to-ceiling windows was the rolling Pacific Ocean lit by a spectacular sunset. I alternated between watching Stefon and staring out the massive picture windows at the salmon and gold sky, the wisps of clouds, and the vast, blue-grey ocean below. All of it framed in floor-length rust curtains. An osprey dove into the waves and emerged, huge wings flapping, fish in its beak.

The first wall had an opening to the hallway and front door, and the kitchen entry, which was flanked by open space over a live-edge wood breakfast bar that separated the white, wood, and metal kitchen from the rest of the living space.

My mountain of a boyfriend is just as tall, dark, and handsome as Uncle Cyrus, but those were about the only things they have in common. Stefon Grant—aka Stefon Stone Cleaver—is a big, nerdy guy with a lush dark beard and a full head of tight curls in a brown so rich it's almost black. His eyes are equally dark, and his lips? Well. We'll talk about those bad boys later. He's a knight with the Society for Medieval Anachronism, a crackerjack computer programmer, and a gaming geek extraordinaire. He's also a sexy, muscular, Black man. One of the reasons he says he likes me is for my size. While I'm not nearly as muscular or big as he is—and am paler than the full moon—I'm what people often call Amazonian. Whatever it is he likes about me, I'm glad it works.

Stefon spends his very good income on electronic equipment, medieval gear for his hobby as a knight with his local chapter of the SMA, and a portfolio of investments that I'm not certain of. His regular—or mundane, as he and his friends call it—clothing is run-of-the-mill geek. When he's not in medieval garb, Stefon lives in a uniform of jeans or cargo pants and some sort of T-shirt. Sometimes he dresses the ensemble up with a blazer, though, this being Seashell Cove, that's rare. This evening's outfit was no exception. He wore faded jeans, sheepskin-lined black slippers, a "Sisko is My Captain" T-shirt, and an open black hoodie with a flaming, twenty-sided die embroidered on the back.

I'm not kidding when I say Stefon's place is fancy. The cottage I inherited from my dad was cozy and comfy, whereas Stefon's place was high end. The two-bedroom apartment had creamy walls decorated with medieval-style artwork in frames I couldn't afford. A giant television and gaming console commanded the wall above a gas fireplace. I had a hard time even calling the sleek black rectangle a fireplace, given that it was the kind you turn on with the flick of a switch, unlike mine, which requires a stack of wood and some patience to get going.

So yeah, Stefon's apartment is a lot more upscale than the cozy house I inherited from Dad, but he's made it a comfortable place all the same. And while I might have more square footage, I'll never have these views.

Stefon and I have been dating for just going on a year, and I've only recently become comfortable with using the B word.

I'm not sure what it was that made me so skittish about calling him my boyfriend, other than my life had been so erratic and filled with a lot of personal difficulties since I moved back to Seashell Cove. I'd midwifed my father through his death, and now I just needed to focus on running the bookstore.

And getting tested by the super-secret council of warlocks and witches. That's my name for it. I have no idea what the organization is actually called, and my uncle Cyrus isn't telling me. Just because the person who tested me ended up trying to kill me, and had killed a dryad, didn't mean I had failed, thank the Gods.

But undergoing those tests bought me face-to-face with the fact that I'd been avoiding my legacy as not only a magical detective, but a capital-J Justice.

I'm still figuring out what all of that means, but having a knight for a boyfriend is actually helpful on that front.

Knights are fond of talking about things like honor and justice.

"What are you making?" I asked. The smells emerging from Stefon's small kitchen were enticing.

"Just a chicken veggie stir-fry," he said. "And some rice. Do you need more wine?"

I thought about it and decided yes, what the heck. I was spending the night and didn't have to drive anywhere.

"Sure."

"Why don't you come sit at the bar and tell me more about this case."

I picked up my wine glass and padded across the rust and black woven Moroccan rug in the slippers I kept at his apartment. Oh, Stefon had been dancing around us living together too, but I was thoroughly avoiding that conversation. So far. One thing at a time, right?

I plunked my glass down on the breakfast bar that separated the kitchen from the rest of the living space and scooched up onto one of the high bar chairs that were suited for my frame, which isn't always usual.

Sure enough, Stefon was flipping the amazing smelling food inside an old, battered wok on the gas flames of his shiny stainless-steel stove. For a medievalist, he sure did like fancy new gadgets. I guess that was the computer geek part of him.

He banged the spatula on the side of the wok and set it on a spoon rest, then turned toward the matching stainless-steel refrigerator and emerged with the bottle of white wine we were working our way through. He leaned over and gave me a sweet kiss on the lips before pouring me more wine.

"So, you think it's a centaur?"

I shrugged, tasting the Oregon Pinot Grigio, a light, crisp wine that was a favorite of mine when the weather started to warm.

"It seems like it," I said, "but I'm not a hundred-percent sure. I mean, first off, why would a centaur want to kill a pixie? And second, I've only heard stories about the centaurs outside of town. I've never actually seen one."

"Just because you haven't seen something," he started, taking a sip of his own wine and gesturing with the glass.

"...doesn't mean it doesn't exist," I finished.

He smirked, poured himself more wine, then turned the heat down under the stir fry, giving it one last swirl with the spatula before covering it.

"What do you know about centaurs?" he asked.

"Well..." I considered the question. "Their magic is different than witches' magic, that's for sure, and it's also different from the nature spirits I'm used to dealing with."

"In what way?" He leaned on the counter across from me and stroked a finger across my forearm.

"Well, the nature spirits... Their magic has a specific purpose. Same with the household beings like the hobs and all that."

"Like Toby?"

"Yeah, like Toby."

Toby is a hob that's partnered with my ex-girlfriend Cecilia. There'd been some trouble with Toby and some garden spirits a few months back, but they all seemed okay now.

"And the centaurs?" Stefon asked, before turning

back to the stir-fry. He poked in some chopsticks, popped a piece of chicken in his mouth, and nodded, seeming to decide it was done. He flipped the gas flame off and reached up for plates.

"Centaur magic is frankly something I need to learn more about," I said. "Can I help?"

"I've got it. You can do the dishes." That was our usual arrangement anyway, because Stefon was a better cook than I am.

He scooped fragrant rice from the small rice cooker.

"I might have to ask Uncle Cyrus for help. Or dig through my parent's library."

"You know I'm always down for research," he said. "And I bet Tabitha and Tracy would be thrilled."

I didn't know whether to smile or groan at that. The teens loved to research into all things magical, paranormal, and spooky. I had to admit they'd been a big help to me so far.

"Good idea. I'll let the teens loose on the problem. But meanwhile?"

"What's up, babe?" Stefon asked, placing a beautiful plate of fluffy white rice, golden-brown chicken, and bright multicolored vegetables in front of me. He also set down chopsticks and a napkin for each of us.

"Can we not talk about this anymore tonight? I think my brain needs a break."

"You got it, babe." And then he gave me another kiss and sat down.

That's why he's my boyfriend. He's handsome, he can cook, and he knows when to leave well enough alone.

7

M y little orange Fiat zipped down the curving road, heading slightly north and east. I was heading into the woods outside of town, and doing something even I knew was foolish.

Centaur hunting. It was surely going to get me an ass-kicking—literally or figuratively—from someone.

Two someones in particular: Uncle Cyrus or Stefon.

Not being foolish enough to head off without telling anyone where I was going—Hello? I've watched horror movies on rainy Saturday nights—I had messaged Stefon. He sent a frantic message back, telling me to wait for him, but I couldn't.

So yeah, he was going to be angry. Uncle Cyrus was going to be angry.

And now that I thought about it, the teenagers were also going to be angry. Not because I was putting myself in danger, but because I'd left them out of such an exciting venture.

I took a curve, one hand on the wheel, the other

snagging my sunglasses from the visor. Until I hit the deep woods, the spring sun was throwing off enough glare for me to squint.

Usually, it was Cecilia who was pissed at me about something, but she was on a "staycation" with her sweetheart, Toby the hob. It seemed strange to take time off work and not see your friends, but I guess Toby had requested some one-on-one time, so I was giving them space.

So, one less person to kick my ass, though the centaurs themselves might do me the favor.

If I could even find them.

The sun began its westering dance over the ocean as I headed further east, down the winding highway, past the the tribal casino, and deeper into the woods. The green rose on either side of the road, the sunlight flashing off and on like a strobe light in one of the Portland night clubs where Cecilia and I used to dance our nights away. Most of the cars were heading in the opposite direction, toward the ocean rather than away.

Sunset chasers.

I couldn't blame them. I would rather be at the fancy hotel bar, enjoying a glass of wine and a plate of truffle fries with my boyfriend instead of facing down a possibly dangerous and angry herd of centaurs.

I wasn't sure where to even look for them. Where did horse people hang out? I'd only heard stories about them, but never met one. The hoofprints in The Kelpie's garden were the first actual sign I'd seen that they really existed.

I was counting on my witch's intuition to kick in and lead the way.

My phone buzzed from the cup holder between the seats. I glanced down and grabbed it. Stefon. Engaging the Bluetooth, I answered, even though that was against my better judgment.

"You're already going, aren't you?"

"What? No greeting? No hello, how was your day?"

"Come on, Sarah, I asked you that earlier. Right before I asked you to wait for me." Yep. He was grumpy and annoyed.

"I was too antsy," I replied, keeping my eyes on the hairpin turns. Not only did I not want to crash into another car on the narrow two-lane stretch, I didn't want to hit an animal darting from the trees. My little electric steed couldn't take on a raccoon, let alone the more likely deer.

"I have to go, Stefon," I said, jerking my wheel to avoid a protruding root ball jutting into the side of my lane. "I can't drive this road and talk at the same time."

"If something bad happens to you, I'll kill you." His sigh telegraphed a whole host of things he wasn't saying out loud. And when had I developed the ability to read his sighs for subtext?

"Duly noted," I replied. "Talk to you later, okay?" All of a sudden I desperately wanted things to be okay with Stefon.

"Talk to you later," he replied. "Please stay safe."

"Will do." I disconnected the call.

Fear trickled down my spine. The tall trees, which I loved, did not seem so welcoming today. The farther I drove into the gloom of green and brown, the more my shoulders threatened to hunch up under my ears again.

I rolled my shoulders, then my neck, and relaxed my grip on the steering wheel.

"What are you doing, Sarah?" I asked myself.

"Indeed," said a dry, smooth voice next to me. "What are you doing, Sarah?"

I slammed on the brakes and whipped my head to the side, where my dapper uncle Cyrus sat, face looking like a storm, smelling of incense and Bay Rum.

"Damn it!" I said, starting down the road again. Thank the Gods and Goddesses no one was behind me.

Even angry, Uncle Cyrus was one of the most beautiful warlocks I'd ever seen.

We weren't related by blood, but he'd been part of my family since I could remember. In contrast to my fish-belly white skin and serviceable clothing, Uncle Cyrus was a Black man who my quick glance showed wore crisp dark blue jeans and equally crisp lavender shirt with the cuffs rolled up to an exacting position on his forearms, beneath the pushed-up sleeves of a light white sweater. As usual, silver glinted from his fingers and diamond earrings winked from his earlobes.

"You could've made me crash," I said, focusing on the curving road.

"You were already in danger. What in the name of all the Gods and Goddesses were you thinking?"

"I thought the council decided I had passed my tests and was a full-fledged whatever I need to be," I groused. "I thought you didn't need to check up on me anymore."

"As long as my niece is off doing foolish things, I'm always going to check up on her."

I exhaled noisily, bumping down the suddenly too-small road.

"Funny," I said, "I thought taking on the mantle of Justice meant I was supposed to do things like oh, investigate possible suspects after a magical creature was killed. And I might I remind you there's a dead human too."

"Police ruled that death accidental. Heart attack."

That was a piece of information I didn't know. "Seriously?"

He just shrugged.

"That shrug tells me you don't believe it," I said, looking for a place to turn off. A flicker dove across the roadway, the watery light flashing on the orange tips of its wings.

"Oh, I believe it was a heart attack. I'm just not sure it wasn't magically induced."

"Seriously?" I said again.

He just gave me one of those looks as if to say I was a naïve fool. And I supposed I was. There was just so much I had avoided looking at during the years of taking care of my father as he died. And then more time trying to get my stuff together afterwards. Trying to figure out how to make a small book and gift shop in a mostly sleepy touristy seaside town profitable for another twenty years.

I sure as heck didn't like to think about people killing other people with magic.

I found a small opening to my left, a clearing between two hemlock trees. I stopped the car and stepped out to breathe in the fresh forest air.

Uncle Cyrus stepped out too, carefully shutting the

door of my little electric Fiat. He frowned down at the bright orange paint.

"Not exactly well camouflaged, are you?"

I shrugged, irritated he was here, irritated I was glad he was here, and really irritated that he was right. I had bought the orange car to ward off the inevitable January blues that happened on the Oregon coast, but now wondered if it was a bad choice for someone with a new career as a magical detective.

"Well, it's what I've got. If you feel like paying to get it repainted, I'm sure Cecilia can give us a good deal."

He smirked at me, knowing I hated it when he gave me extravagant gifts, but also knowing I was just annoyed enough to accept it.

"Where to?" he asked.

I looked around, trying to think. If I were a centaur, where would I live? I stepped into the forest's edge, shuffled my boots in the soft loam beneath me, and sent a tendril of energy down, connecting to the spirit of the place.

Every place has its own spirit, and every rock and tree is connected to that spirit of the place, along with having their own spirits.

Hi, I'm Sarah, I thought, by way of introduction. Not that the spirit would notice me, but it just felt rude to not say anything.

I took in a deep breath and struggled for a moment before finding my center. I breathed in, then up and out, opening my senses to the space around me. To the familiar scent of Bay Rum and frankincense that was Uncle Cyrus. To the slight ticking sound the car was making. To the calling of that flicker, and the smaller cheeping twitters of chickadees joined by the squawking of a jay.

I couldn't hear any gulls here. The trees muffled the sound from the ocean.

I wasn't sure exactly what I was seeking out, just a sense of direction. A way to go. Something pinged in my solar plexus.

"That way," I said, pointing towards a small pathway leading southwest, through the forest and in the general direction of the cliffs above the sea.

8

————

Uncle Cyrus's navy-blue wingtips crunched over a dead twig. I glanced down at his completely inappropriate footwear, and then at my black hiking boots. I swear, Cyrus was never dressed appropriately for Seashell Cove, but he always seem to look perfect anyway.

"Aren't you worried you're going to mess up your shoes?"

He just raised an eyebrow and kept walking.

"Right," I muttered, "Mr. I'm-Too-Perfect Warlock."

I heard him snort, and had to grin despite myself.

"So," he said, glancing over his shoulder, "you felt something this way? Centaurs?"

I hurried to catch up with his longer stride. I'm not small myself, and my long legs and sturdy muscles are usually able to keep up with anyone, but I swear Uncle Cyrus is preternaturally swift. And that reminded me, Stefon and I hadn't been jogging in a week. And with weather this good? That was just a crying shame.

"All I know is something pinged me from this direction. I've never met a centaur, so it's hard for me to gauge whether it feels like them or not."

Cyrus sniffed delicately at the air.

"I smell horses over there," he said, and veered in a slightly more westerly direction. We walked in silence for a little while before Cyrus started to speak again.

"I know you don't like me interfering, but I'm truly surprised that you came out here alone."

I started to object and he lifted a hand to stop me.

"I understand you think you need to do things on your own because you're the current magical Justice, but that's just not true. We all need help."

"Even you?" Uncle Cyrus asking anyone for anything was a big surprise.

"Of course me," he said, irritation tinging his voice. "What do you think your parents and I did all those years? Sure, we were friends, but that came after."

"Do you mean you worked together?"

"Of course we did. That was how we first met. Before we became close. Before..." He waved his hand. "You know."

Uncle Cyrus had trouble talking about his feelings. I think I got that, considering I had only just recently started calling Stefon my boyfriend and telling him I loved him and stuff. And it took almost getting taken out by a sorcerer for me to come around to it.

I reached out and touched his white sweater. He turned, and we both paused.

"Hey," I said, keeping my voice gentle, "I get it. I miss them too."

He just nodded, but I could swear there were tears turning his eyes glassy before he blinked them away.

He started walking again.

"I just thought," he said, our feet softly crunching on the forest floor, "that after the events of January you would have a...what do you call it? A squad."

I grinned at that, ducking to avoid a low-hanging fir branch. A squirrel chittered and yelled at us from above.

"Talk to the management," I said, looking up at its wide eyes and thrashing fluffy tail.

"I do have a squad, I guess." I was thinking of the teens, and Stefon, and even Delta Crabbit, weird as she was. "And I'm going to have them work on researching all the rest. But I just thought..."

"You just thought you would come out into the middle of the forest to search for creatures you've never met before who may or may not have killed someone?"

Since he was correct, I didn't even bother to reply. I just kept walking.

"I sense something." And sure enough, there was a shimmering of white on the bark of a spruce tree.

"Centaur tail hair," Uncle Cyrus said.

I reached out.

"Don't touch it!"

I stopped, my fingers hovering bare inches away from the silky-looking strands.

"Which way?" he said. He was letting me take lead, which was good, even though he could've found them much faster than I could, I was sure.

"Continue west. Toward your right."

He held out a hand and bowed slightly as if to usher me ahead.

As we walked, I refocused my breathing, the way I had been taught. Trying to open my senses and feel what might be around. I had to admit I was enjoying walking with Cyrus. And I wished more than anything that I was truly just out on a pleasant forest walk with my favorite adopted uncle. Except, Cyrus was not usually one for walking in the woods. He only did so when he was on a case like this, or under some duress.

No. My memories of walking in the forest? They were all memories of my father.

I swallowed back the tears building at the back of my throat and worked to call my thoughts back. To breathe slowly and deeply. Trying to sense what was beyond the edges of my skin.

I could feel the strange magic all around me now, and start to smell it, too. A subtle scent of mingled horse and human. The pathway wound around, growing closer to the ocean. I could hear the gulls now, and hear the faint crashing of the waves. The air changed suddenly, and a scent of brine swept through, mingling with the citrusy-pine scent of hemlock, and the fresh clean scent of fir.

And through the trees I saw flashes of white. The same iridescent white as the strands of tail. There was also shimmering rainbow black, and a deep rich brown. All flashing through the trees as we walked.

I paused and whispered, "What do we do?"

"You step forward and you greet the ones who live here." The new voice was deep and rumbling. I gasped and turned to my left, my head snapping towards the most beautiful creature I've ever seen in my life.

She had that shimmering rainbow-black hide on a long muscular body. And rising up from the horse body was a small-breasted, dark-skinned human-looking... woman? I wasn't sure if centaurs had a clear gender, or whether they consider themselves women or men or something else.

Uncle Cyrus bowed next to me, and after a few seconds, I followed suit.

"Our apologies," Uncle Cyrus said. "My niece and I do not mean to intrude."

"And yet you walk our lands," the centaur replied. But even though the voice was calm, a steely challenge undergirded it.

I looked into her liquid black eyes, and I swear they were shot through with stars. Taking in a shuddering breath, I sought the feel of my feet and my boots on the ground. I straightened my spine, and forced myself to hold the starry gaze.

"And?" she asked, raising a peaked eyebrow.

Keeping my breath as steady as I could, I spoke. "A pixie was killed outside The Historic Kelpie Inn. A human, too. We sensed a centaur nearby the scene and came to see if you knew anything about this, or could help."

She threw back her head and laughed.

"Why in the world would a centaur wish to harm a pixie?" Her face clouded again. "Are you accusing us?"

Though her voice remained calm, I was suddenly afraid. Afraid, and glad Uncle Cyrus had butted in and invited himself along.

"We do not mean to cause offense," Uncle Cyrus said.

"And yet you do. Humans always do, which is why we avoid you. Oh, even those of you who consider your-self more than human." The centaur practically spat the word out.

Yeah. Maybe coming here hadn't been such a bright idea.

But what other choice did I really have?

9

The heat of anger replaced my fear. If I was going to act as Justice, I had to be able to talk to magical creatures without fearing I was going to get kicked or bitten.

"I don't know what I expected when I came here," I said, "but I didn't expect to be insulted by you. And I certainly didn't expect you to insult my uncle."

"And why shouldn't I insult you?" The centaur drew her shoulders back. "You come here, to our Grove, and start asking about dead pixies?"

Uncle Cyrus stepped forward as if to intervene, but I turned my shoulders to block him just slightly. He could still get around me if he wanted to, but it was clear I was the one talking to her now.

"A human is dead. And so is a pixie. And hoofprints were found near where they both died."

"And how do you know it wasn't just a horse?"

"It smelled like magic." I widened my stance and stood even taller, moving my shoulders back to match the centaur's posture. Not for the first time, I was grateful for my Amazonian frame. I could almost look the centaur eye to eye.

"It smelled like magic, and the hoofprints were not deep enough to be a horse and a rider both."

Arms crossed over her chest, the centaur paused and pawed at the ground with one hoof, as if thinking.

"Follow me." She whirled, showing us her luxuriant tail, and headed down the path.

I looked at Uncle Cyrus, who just shrugged and started walking. I followed.

It wasn't long before I saw the most magical thing I've ever encountered in my life. If this was what being a magical Justice meant, maybe it would be okay. Those flashes I had seen earlier?

Yeah. They were centaurs. Black, brown, and white. All of them one solid color, shimmering in the sunlight. What I thought of as the human parts of them were colored just slightly differently than the hide on the horse parts. But white matched to white, brown matched brown, and black matched black. All of them were mind-bogglingly beautiful.

Uncle Cyrus stopped in his tracks, and I heard him murmur softly, "Oh, my."

I sidled up next to him. "You've never met centaurs either?"

He shook his head. "No, they keep to themselves."

The black centaur stopped beside us then. "We have our reasons."

I don't know why I kept thinking of her as a she, other than the slightly feminine torso. I would have to ask about gender later, when I wasn't risking offending her at every moment.

The centaurs all stopped and turned, one by one, to stare at us as we walked forward behind the first centaur. I was kicking myself for not asking her name. But this whole situation had made me so off kilter, I simply forgotten introductions. What was even stranger was that Uncle Cyrus had, too. He was usually such a stickler for protocol.

"Come forth," the first centaur said. "These humans have questions for us."

A majestic white horse with a human male torso and ice-blue eyes trotted forward. He tossed his head, and a silky fall of white hair fell across his shoulders. I stifled a laugh. It was such a stereotypical popular-girl move, and seeing it on such a powerful creature struck me as funny.

"Who are they to question anything we do?" he asked, trotting around us, examining us as if we were bugs under a microscope. "And how did they find our meadow, anyway?"

He finished his circuit and faced me head-on, raising one imperious eyebrow. It seemed centaurs were fond of the old eyebrow raise.

I shrugged. Two could play the I'm-a-jerk game.

"It really wasn't hard." I crossed my arms over my chest. "You actually think this place is hidden?"

Several centaurs snorted and pawed at the ground, and Uncle Cyrus touched my arm in warning. But I was still angry.

I raised my voice to carry across the meadow, because even though I knew one of these creatures could kill me with a carefully placed strike of their gleaming, sharp, hooves, I wasn't going to let them stop me either. The dead human—heart attack or not—and the drained pixie were counting on me.

"A pixie is dead," I said. My voice rang strong and true across the grassy area. "And a human is dead, too. We found prints that we think came from a centaur around the area."

"And you dare accuse us?" A voice shouted, but I didn't see which centaur it came from.

"Careful," Uncle Cyrus muttered. But he was letting me handle it, which was good.

"We are simply asking," I replied. "Seeking information."

A dozen pairs of eyes stared at us as the sun shone in the clearing, making their hair—manes?—and bodies glisten. If it were any other situation, I would've been asking one million questions about their magic, and whether I could pet them, or if that was offensive... But here we were. So I waited. And they waited. A standoff.

Okay. Clearly, they weren't going to offer up any information on their own.

"The sooner you answer, the sooner we leave," I said, and then the waiting game began again. There was another snort or two, but no one said a word. My stomach growled. Great, good time to get hungry, Sarah.

"And if you don't answer our questions," I said, a wild thought bursting in my head, "I know a lot of children in Seashell Cove who will be thrilled to meet you." Not that I would ever follow through on placing children near such clearly dangerous creatures. But the centaurs didn't need to know that.

The white centaur snapped his teeth at me.

"You dare..." he said. The first centaur held about a hand to stop him.

"No threats, human," she said, taking two steps toward me.

"Look," I said, not backing down, "a magical creature is dead. Does that mean anything to you?"

Again, with the blank stares, and where I still saw anger, there was also something else. Some uncertainty.

"I think you know something but you're not telling us. And I want you to know that withholding information only hurts us all. I'm on your side."

"That's what you Justices always say," a brown centaur said. She trotted forward, eyes flashing. "I have worked with you witches before, you Justices, and where did it get us? Nowhere. Promises were made and not kept."

Uncle Cyrus cleared his throat. "I think I know what happened." His voice was tinged with sadness.

"And what is that?" The brown centaur asked sharply, waiting.

"The person who entered into those agreements with you is dead. Killed by a traitor."

"How do we know you are not lying?" said the white centaur with the flowing hair.

"You don't," I replied with a sigh. "Now, we will be on our way."

I was suddenly not only angry and frightened, I was heartsick too. I couldn't take any more of this.

"Let's go, Uncle Cyrus." I turned to leave.

"Wait." Surprisingly, it was the white centaur who spoke. He conferred with the black and the brown centaurs in low, urgent tones. I could clearly hear words forming, but didn't understand what they were saying. Apparently, centaurs had a language all their own.

Uncle Cyrus moved closer to me, which gave me some comfort.

Finally, the conference ended, and the black centaur held my gaze again.

"We may have information," she said, "but we're not certain of it. One of us will come to you at dusk within the next three days. Be alert. Remain ready."

I bit down my irritation at her authoritative tone. This was as good as it was going to get, and that was clear.

"Thank you. I will be ready."

And then, finally, Uncle Cyrus and I turned to go, though I had to admit, turning my back on the centaurs made me nervous. I had to force myself to keep my eyes trained on the path ahead.

But I could feel them. Watching.

10

I sat at a blond wood four top in Angie's Blueberry Café with Uncle Cyrus, Delta Crabbit, and Preston, a chubby, white cheeked, white bearded gnome who sported a blue cap with purple embroidery. Preston was a cranky creature, but he and Delta seemed to get along just fine.

Of course, Delta tended toward the cranky herself, so maybe they had an affinity.

The murmur of conversations, the hiss of steam from the cappuccino machine, and the clink of teaspoons on mugs made a musical counterpoint to the Lizzo bumping through the café speakers. That was one thing I liked about Angie's place—the music was real.

A blueberry muffin sat in front of me, and my usual cup of English Breakfast tea was close to hand. Uncle Cyrus sipped espresso across the table from me, and to my right and left, Delta and the gnome drank hot chocolate piled with whipped cream.

My muffin was perfect, warm, with just the right amount of crusty top and just the right level of sweet. I should really be eating a sandwich, but it was hard to eat and talk at the same time. So, I was making do with chunks from the muffin while we got through this meeting.

Flags and pennants along Main Street snapped in the wind, their bright colors shining in the springtime sun. The big dino skeleton head grinned from down the way, and I wondered how Tetris was doing. I should stop by the fossil shop and ask why I hadn't seen him around lately.

More than anything, I wanted to be jogging on the beachfront with Stefon, breathing in the salty air, soothed by the sound of the waves, but apparently there was a crime to solve.

I turn to the gnome, who was propped up on a booster seat sipping at his tiny cup of hot chocolate.

"Have you heard anything about this?" I asked, eyes riveted on the cream slowly dripping down his beard. Delta motioned to his face and made a wiping motion. He blotted his mouth with a napkin, which only succeeded in smearing the whipped cream further.

"Oh, the gnomes are talking about it all right," he said. "Chaneques and hobs, too. Everyone's right terrified."

"But do they have any information?" Uncle Cyrus sniffed, then took another sip of his espresso, pinkie raised. He was always so proper, and dang well put together.

The gnome scowled at him. "You high and mighty

warlocks, you're supposed to be so smart. Why don't you figure it out?"

Great start to the meeting.

"Uncle Cyrus wasn't intending to insult you." I glared at my uncle and then turned back to the gnome. "We're just worried, is all. And we need as much help as we can get."

"That's a good thing," Delta Crabbit said. "A Justice should work *for* all the beings and *with* all the beings, not go off like some lone gun in an old Western."

Now it was her turn to glare at Uncle Cyrus.

He set down his espresso cup with a click and raised both his hands in surrender.

"I understand that, Delta, and you of all people know that I do," he said. "Just as I understand there's a new sheriff in town who does things differently. I'm just here to offer her support."

I stifled a grin and then got back to business. Angie stopped by the table, a damp white rag in hand.

"Anything?" she asked. Angie's blond hair was tied back with a blueberry-blue kerchief that matched the apron she wore over jeans, a white T-shirt, and those clogs that all restaurant workers seem to like.

"Not yet." I sighed. "The centaurs know something but aren't telling, and the police have declared the opera singer's death is from natural causes."

I shoved a large bite of muffin in my mouth and chewed before I could say something I shouldn't.

"Sarah Braxton!"

I groaned. Chip Lancaster flounced through the café, trench coat and baggy jeans flapping, pasty face set in a scowl. He loomed over my chair.

"Chip, what have I told you about bothering my customers?" Angie asked.

"The public has a right to know…"

"The right to know exactly what, Chip? I didn't kill anyone. The police have closed the case. Natural causes." Not that I believed that but, hey, if it got rid of Chip Lancaster, I wasn't above a little prevarication.

He sneered. "You know that isn't all there is to the story, and mark my words, I'm going to ferret. It. Out."

He looked a bit like a ferret in that moment, but I prudently didn't say that.

"You do that, Chip." I kept my voice mild. Chip's eyes bugged out.

Huh. Maybe Uncle Cyrus was onto something with that whole cool-as-a-cucumber bit.

"You!" Chip wagged a pasty finger my way, almost smacking me with his trench coat sleeve.

"Enough!" Angie growled, stepping between Chip and my chair. "You need to leave."

"I am a journalist…!"

"Now." Angie crossed her arms over her impressive chest and glared. Chip sniffed and whirled around, then flapped through the café, slamming open the door.

Angie sighed, then pulled a chair next to Delta and plopped her sturdy frame down. She was another strapping woman like myself, and gorgeous to boot. But she always said she didn't have time for love, being too busy running the Blueberry Café. I think there was a deeper story there, but we weren't close enough friends for me to push. Yet.

"There's something that's been bothering me...." she said.

We all just waited. I sipped my milky tea, then took another bite of muffin, the blueberry taste bursting between my teeth.

When Angie looked up, her eyes were haunted. "I've suspected something's going on at The Kelpie for quite some time. Liam has seemed extra distracted lately. As if he has something going on at the inn that he doesn't want to talk about."

Interesting. I knew they were friends and colleagues, like most of local businesspeople in a small town, but it sounded like they might also be something more. So much for Angie not having time for love.

"Any idea what it is?" I asked.

"I don't know," she said. "But I do know the last time I was there dropping off morning muffins for their guests..." She paused again and looked out the window.

"Angie." I grabbed her hand. "Just spit it out."

She looked around, making sure none of the other customers were listening. Then leaned over the table.

"A couple of the ghosts seemed agitated last time I was there. One of them kept getting in my way when I tried to walk into the kitchen."

Uncle Cyrus grew very still across the table from me.

"Did they tell you what they wanted?" he asked.

Angie shook her head, then slicked off her head scarf, wiped her brow, and carefully retired it.

"No, and that was the strangest thing. I mean, ghosts know that I can see them, right? So sometimes I am their go-to person if no one else is around. But this one…it was the strangest thing." Her eyes got that faraway look as if she was back at The Kelpie, remembering. "I finally had to set the muffins down in the dining room instead of in the kitchen because it kept blocking the door. And I swear it tried to tell me something at least three times but it was as if it couldn't."

"As if it were under a geas?" Uncle Cyrus asked

"Gesh?" I said. "What's that?"

Delta Crabbit and the gnome both *tsked* at me as if I were an uneducated fool.

"You'd better get the teens helping you with more research," Delta muttered.

"Angie? Cyrus?" I asked, ignoring the crotchety witch.

"A geas is either a prohibition or a compulsion," Cyrus replied. "It's a form of small magic that compels a person to either do or not do something."

"Oh! A gey-us! Like in Stefon's role-playing games."

Now it was Cyrus's turn to wince. "Something like that."

Delta snorted. I waved a hand at her and turned back to Angie.

"Sorry to interrupt, Angie. You were saying the ghost wanted to tell you something?"

She nodded. "I don't know what was stopping it. Whether it was a geas or something else. All I know is that it seemed afraid."

If something could cause someone that was already dead to have that kind of fear? I wasn't sure I wanted to get to the bottom of this after all.

11

Much as I wanted to race down to The Historic Kelpie after our breakfast meeting, I really needed to check in at The Widening Gyre. My assistant, Duncan, did excellent work, but as owner of the place, I did need to show up almost every day. Make sure there were no disasters or fires to put out. Uncle Cyrus popped off to who knows where, saying he would talk to me later, and Delta Crabbit and the gnome said they were both going to stay and get more hot chocolate.

Delta also muttered darkly about having things to attend to, and I wasn't sure I wanted to know what she meant. As I walked the few blocks to the bookshop, I glanced up at the large flapping dinosaur skull flag outside Ancient Treasures. I noticed that along with the new display of fossils and crystals, there were several books I hadn't noticed before. Tetris and I had an agreement: he could carry a few fossil-related books, but would send people down the street to my shop for things more directly archaeology- and history-related.

In return, I sent anyone with the slightest interest in fossils, shells, or dinosaurs down to him. I looked more closely at the door, and noticed he had a closed sign in the window.

"Well, that's not right," I said, stopping for a moment on the sidewalk. A stroller-pushing parent let out a mild curse at me as they jerked their stroller around where I was rooted on the sidewalk.

"Sorry," I called after their retreating form. Why in the world would Tetris be closed? It wasn't his usual day off. The shops on Main Street all closed on Mondays during the winter months, but during tourist season we agreed to stay open seven days a week if we could. That was the main reason I hired Duncan. I couldn't really afford him yet, but I also couldn't afford to shut down when there were people milling around, eating ice cream cones and french fries, or going hunting for fishing floats and driftwood on the beach.

I had no time to wonder where Tetris was, though. Maybe later. I hurried down the block, smiling, and skirting around tourists out enjoying the sun. The shop that sold kites was doing a brisk business.

As I opened the glass door to The Widening Gyre, bells chimed and I heard a small thunk as Rhiannon leapt down from the front window display case and came to greet me.

I bent to scratch her furry black head.

"I know, you always require tribute, because food just isn't enough for you, is it?"

She blinked her green eyes at me and then sneezed. I pulled my hand back quickly avoiding the spray of droplets.

"I swear you do that on purpose." She didn't reply. Just licked a paw as if nothing disgusting had just happened.

I looked up and Duncan was smirking at me, pushing his heavy-framed black glasses back up his nose.

"She almost got you," he said.

"Yeah, well, good thing my reflexes are lightning fast." I looked back down at Rhiannon, who had already turned her butt towards me and was walking away.

"Any news?" I asked

"Just that Tracy called, all excited about something. She and Tabitha said they would stop by later."

"They didn't say what it was about?" I flipped through the mail in my cubby behind the counter.

"No. She said something about needing to tell you in person. And the shop phone not being a secure line."

I shook my head. The teens had branched out from their paranormal studies into some things edging towards conspiracy theory. It was a hop, skip, and a jump from UFOs to wiretaps.

Smart teens needed something to entertain themselves, I guessed. And at least they were doing it at my store where I could keep an eye on them.

Tracy's mother, Carol, appreciated it too. I wondered what Tabitha's parents made of all of this. I'd not met them yet.

Since Duncan had things well in hand, I brewed a cup of tea, plopped my size sixteen jeans on the high stool behind the counter, and got to work on the accounts. Not my favorite thing, but needs must.

The day went by quietly, and I finally paused to stretch the kinks out of my back. Picking up my tea mug, I took a sip, and almost spit it back out. Once hot, milky tea gone cold is disgusting.

The door burst open and the two teenagers rushed in.

"Good, you're here!" Tabitha said, her dark eyes alight.

Both teens wore jeans and boots today. Tracy had on a white Sailor Moon T-shirt, and Tabitha wore a black shirt emblazoned with a bright pink pentagram.

I stifled a smile. Despite them being a pain in the ass periodically, I was happy to see them.

"Can you talk?" Tabitha asked, her black bob swirling above her thin shoulders as if it were animated.

"Do you have time?" Tracy chimed in, her own blond hair loose down her back.

I looked around the shop, checking for customers perusing the shelves.

"Shop's empty," Duncan said. "We had a burst of sales at opening, but it's been pretty quiet since."

I tilted my head towards the back, and both teens moved down the center aisle of bookcases. They headed towards what they know is my favorite seating area with the comfy chairs, and a small table beneath the window with a stack of books picked out in stained glass. The space used to hold two chairs, but it had become our de facto meeting spot, so we'd moved some shelves and the space now held four chairs. I followed, and Rhiannon, strangely enough, came with me.

"Shouldn't you be at school?" I asked.

"It's already three o'clock," Tabitha replied.

How had the day gotten away from me? No wonder I was hungry. And had a headache building. One blueberry muffin wasn't enough food, not to get through the whole day. I needed protein. And a vegetable or two. Maybe some water. But that would have to wait.

I slid back into a stuffed armchair covered in burgundy and gold stripes, and looked at their expectant faces. Clearly, they thought they had stumbled onto something big.

"What have you got?" I asked.

"Well," Tabitha said, leaning forward, a small silver sand dollar swinging forward on a delicate chain. "Lupita from our class?" She raised an eyebrow is if I would know who any of her classmates were. I just nodded, and waved a hand so she would continue.

"Well, she said her brother saw a centaur walking down the road above behind The Kelpie at one in the morning. Two days ago."

"And?" Now it was my turn to raise an eyebrow.

She sat back in her chair with a huff. "Don't you see? They could've been the murderer!"

There was a big crash and flurry from the front of the store followed by the sound of feet smacking on the wood floors and a strange squeaking sound.

Delta Crabbit burst her way into our little meeting, cheeks flushed. She braced herself against a bookcase, panting. The big canvas bag slung over her right arm squirmed and thrashed.

"Ms. Crabbit, are you okay?" Tracy asked. "And shouldn't you let the gnome out?"

The canvas bag was swinging wildly.

Delta held up a hand, still panting. "It's really bad."

Clearly the gnome was having none of it and kicked her in the waist.

Scowling, Delta frantically opened the canvas tote bag, and out popped the angry-looking gnome, blue and purple cap askew on his equally flushed round face.

"Why did you have to bounce me so hard?" he asked as he jerked about, finally freeing his limbs from the sack and leaping to the floor. "And what do I have to do to get a cup of tea around here?"

He crossed his little arms over his little chest and looked at each of us in turn, spearing us with his eyes.

"I'll get tea." Tracy leapt up and headed to the kitchen.

"Stop!" I said. The teen halted in her tracks.

"Delta? How urgent is this?"

"Very urgent," she said. "There isn't time for tea."

"What's going on?" Tabitha asked, face scrunched up in question. The stained glass reflected colored light off Delta's face, making her look like some strange abstract painting standing in the middle of my bookshop.

"Liam called, said it's urgent."

"Delta?" I was really getting tired of not knowing what was going on.

"It's the ghosts," she said. "Something is wrong with the ghosts."

I listened for the sound of falling books, but in that moment?

Biff had decided to remain silent as the grave.

12

———————

At the top of the stairs on the second floor of The Kelpie is an old-fashioned parlor. The sitting room is filled with overstuffed couches, cozy chairs with lamps angled just so, stacks of boardgames and books on shelves, and more weird art on the dark walls. Beyond the sitting room is a hallway leading to the rooms and suites.

Legend has it that at one end of the room there was another staircase that used to go up to the third floor, now closed off. It is said that dancers can sometimes be seen streaming up and down the stairs at certain times of the night.

I made a note to not tell the teens about that, or they would want to camp out here. I had enough on my plate already. Liam paced in front of the multipaned windows from overstuffed sofa to overstuffed chair, somehow avoiding barking his shins on the heavy wood coffee table.

The photographs of dead people staring down at

us, which could've been charming, was slightly creepy in the light filtering through lace curtains. A large seascape painted in oils hung over the Chesterfield sofa on the back wall. I alternated between looking at the boat fighting a cresting wave, and Liam pacing. We'd been here for ten minutes, and I still didn't know anything, and was getting pretty impatient with the whole situation.

No one told me that being a magical detective was mostly waiting around for other people to spill the beans.

And what does that phrase even mean? Spill the beans? That was ridiculous.

"Tell them, Liam," Delta finally said. She sat on one end of the long, dark brown Chesterfield sofa, the gnome at her side, kicking his heels beneath the moody seascape. The two teens sat in chairs, Tabitha with her shoes off and legs crossed beneath her, knees bouncing. Tracy drummed the arms of her chair with excitement. I signaled to them both to chill. Tabitha sighed, but stilled her knees. Tracy shrugged and shot me a grin.

I sat on a sofa opposite the coffee table.

"Liam," I said, "why don't you sit down?"

His pacing was making me dizzy. And I really wanted answers.

"I think we just need to talk to the ghosts," he finally blurted out.

The teens exchanged excited glances.

"Who has the best rapport with them?" I asked, trying to move things along.

"That would be Sophie," Liam said, finally pausing.

I knew Sophie vaguely. She was a woman in her

mid-fifties who helped with housekeeping at The Kelpie.

"Is she here today?" I asked.

"I'll go get her."

Liam turned on his heel and stalked out of the room. I looked at Delta, who shrugged.

"He gets that way sometimes," she said. "There's nothing for it."

He soon returned with Sophie, a buxom white woman in old jeans and a kraken T-shirt, wiping her hands on an apron. Her fading, from-a-bottle-red hair was secured in a messy bun.

"You need to talk to ghosts, do you?" she asked, voice sounding like whiskey and cigarettes. Made me wonder if she was ever a singer. I could picture her in a fancy dress standing in front of an old-fashioned microphone. I shook my head, trying to clear it, which caused her to frown.

"You don't want to talk to the ghosts?"

"No! No. Sorry. I do. We can really use your help."

"Well," she said, looking around the room. "Won't do much good sitting in here. They are all upstairs right now."

Liam frowned and Delta shuddered.

"What's wrong?" Tabitha beat me to the question.

"We closed it up for a reason," Liam muttered, but then started down the stairs.

"Where are we going?" Tracy asked, bouncing to her feet.

"The only access is outside," Sophie said. "Follow me."

We tripped down through the popcorn-scented

lobby, past the porch shark, and around the outside of the building to the side courtyard. And sure enough, hidden behind a massive metal sculpture was a staircase. I hadn't ever really noticed it before, just figuring it was a fire escape of some sort. Liam clambered up the metal stairway, shoes ringing on each step, and we all followed quickly behind. Finally, with some huffing and puffing from the people who did not regularly go beach jogging, we reached the third floor. I turned and looked at the spectacular view of town and mountains. We were on the wrong side to see the ocean, but it was beautiful all the same.

Liam rattled a key in an ancient-looking lock and shouldered open a door that squealed as if it were in pain. And then he disappeared into the darkness.

I stumbled across the threshold, pausing for a moment to let my eyes adjust to the lack of light. Tracy bumped into my back.

"Sorry," we both said. I took another step in, feeling my way forward until finally, from somewhere across the room, Liam switched on a single floor lamp. It had an orange beaded shade and cast a ruddy light in a circle that pooled around the edges of a broad, Art Deco–era rug. A padded rocker sat on one edge of the rug, half in shadow.

The chair was rocking.

Faint strains of scratchy music came from a Victrola on a cabinet against the wall.

And then I heard the dancing. A tapping and sliding across wood floors.

"Most of them are farther back," Sophie said. "But we can talk to this one first, if you like."

"In the rocker?" Tabitha squeaked. Sophie just nodded and headed towards the chair.

My heart jumped in my chest and my hands felt clammy.

Dealing with Biff at the bookstore was one thing, but Biff didn't creep me out like this. In the back of my mind I wondered why, but that was the only coherent thought I had. The rest of me just wanted to run.

I let Sophie approach, hanging back with the teens. Delta and the gnome had disappeared into the shadows somewhere, and Liam was back to his pacing, which was really starting to annoy me. I mean, I get that the guy was freaked out, but I really wished he would stop already.

We all deal with stress in our own ways, I guessed. But not all of us were so annoying. As I stepped slowly toward the suddenly quiet chair, I really wished that Uncle Cyrus was here to help.

Or that Stefon was beside me. I could really stand to hold someone's hand.

13

"Oh. They left," Sophie said, stopping suddenly.

"The rocker ghost?" Tracy squeaked. Sophie just nodded.

Good, I didn't want to talk to what looked like an empty chair anyway. It kind of creeped me out.

I stepped farther into the room and saw shimmering along the back wall. The bar in the here-and-now was a battered old wooden thing that clearly had once been beautiful. Behind it, the glass was antiqued with age, striped and stippled with black and blue and silver. The shelves to either side were empty. But overlaid on top of it all was the bar-that-was.

I could just make out the glow of lights in their Art Deco sconces, setting rows of bottles aglow. There were men in tuxedos or dark suits, and women in fringed and beaded dresses.

Sophie looked strangely out of place in her apron and jeans as she navigated through the dancers, somehow not passing through any of their ghostly bodies. I guess that was a good skill to have if you could talk to ghosts. It was kind of amazing watching the dancers. I never really saw Biff at the bookstore, other than sometimes out of the corner of my eye, I would catch him shuffling along in his old ratty, striped cardigan. But as soon as I tried to look directly at him, he disappeared again. Mostly, Biff manifested by throwing books to get my attention.

But these ghosts? These ghosts were for real.

Sophie approached one of the women at the bar, the one who looked as if she had blond hair once upon a time, set in those amazingly fluid Marcel waves, cropped to her chin. I couldn't really tell exactly what color her gown had been, maybe a royal blue? A chevron pattern made of spangles and beads spilled down the fabric, ending at a handkerchief hem that skimmed somewhere between her knees and her elegant T-strap shoes. Her mouth was elaborately painted in a cupid's bow and at first, she smiled at Sophie, then frowned.

Sophie gestured towards me, and the flapper nodded. The ghost and Sophie both approached me, so I stayed put at I was on the edge of the dance floor.

"Let's head toward the chairs near the window," Sophie said, and led the way to a whole other area I hadn't noticed before. Where the sofas and chairs on the floor below were the overstuffed kind from the nineteen-forties, this furniture was slicker. More streamlined.

Why there was a whole Art Deco nightclub above The Kelpie, I didn't know. I always thought of speakeasies as being in basements. I didn't trust the situation enough to sit down on any of furniture—it looked solid, but who really knew?—but the ghost had no compunction about that. She perched elegantly on a tufted chair, crossing her ankles one over the other and setting a cigarette into a long holder. So, not only did they dance and drink alcohol, apparently ghosts smoked cigarettes too.

::*All right, what do you want to know?*::

In for a penny...

"Delta tells me some of the ghosts here were upset about something. Does that happen to be related to the death of the opera singer in the garden? Or the pixie?"

The ghost looked troubled. Was that guilt that flashed across her face? It was hard to tell. She kept shimmering just in and out of focus.

The ghost took a long drag on the cigarette holder, her polished nails winking in the dim lights. She gestured and said something I didn't catch, but I could tell from the look on Sophie's face that it wasn't anything good. Tracy and Tabitha crept closer, hovering near me, but they kept quiet.

I strained, trying to hear the ghost's response over the music, laughter, and Liam's steady pacing. You'd think since her voice was inside my head, I'd be able to...but then, I guess the music must be in my head, too. Liam's pacing, however? He was really getting on my nerves and making it hard to concentrate. I really wished he would just go outside.

I inhaled through my nose and out through my mouth as slowly as I could, trying to calm my nerves, and then I focused on the area on my forehead some people call the third eye, imagining I could send a breath through that. Maybe activating my extra senses would help me tune into the ghost better.

The lights turned up. The music grew louder, and then yes, Liam's pacing increased in tempo. Great, I had just made things worse.

::...person in a trench coat.::

Wait a minute. I could hear the ghost now. My psychic tuning trick had worked.

"What did she say about a person in a trench coat?" I slid closer to Sophia and the ghost. Sophie's arms were crossed over her chest, her mouth turned down.

The gramophone squawked as clumsy hands lifted the needle to change a record.

"She said she and one other ghost saw some things through the windows that night. They saw the singer, and then a person in a trench coat."

"How about a centaur or a pixie?"

The flapper shrugged and took a long drag on her cigarette again.

Now that my psychic senses were open, I could smell the acrid bite of it in the air, along with the scent of whiskey and some sort of fruity drinks.

::There did seem to be brightness fluttering around the trench coat person's head. It may have been a pixie, or perhaps not. Hard to tell.::

"Can you ask any of the others?" I said. "Please, it's important."

The ghost tilted her head and then shrugged before rising and walking away. I could hear the heels of her T-strap shoes clicking on the wood floors.

"What do you think?" I asked Sophie.

Now it was Sophie's turn to shrug. There was too

much shrugging going on, as far as I was concerned. The housekeeper sat down on the loveseat. It seemed solid enough to hold her, so I sat down at her side.

"It's hard to tell with these ghosts. Sometimes they're coherent, and sometimes they're not. I don't know if it depends on the phase of the moon and the tides, or their age, or the season. I've tried to find a pattern, but I haven't yet."

"How long have you worked here?" Tracy asked.

"Off and on for four years. It's just part-time, while I take care of my grandkids. I'm also a part-time book-keeper for a couple of local businesses."

That's the way things went in small tourist towns. A lot of people have to cobble together a living. Especially those of us who live in the "not a view" neighborhoods.

I looked around. The flapper ghost was dancing. Just great.

"Do you think she's coming back?"

"Your guess is as good as mine," Sophie said.

"If she takes more than three more minutes, I'm going after her," I replied. Turning, I caught Liam's eye and motioned him toward us. The man looked terri-fied, as if he might run outside at any moment and throw up.

He approached me warily, as if I were a ghost instead of just a bookseller trying to figure out what the heck was going on in this town.

When had I become someone that people were afraid of? That was a question to ponder for another day. For now, we had ghost to wrangle.

"Liam, did you know this? About the ghosts seeing a person in a trench coat?"

"The ghosts say they see a lot of things," he replied, raking stiff fingers through his brown hair. "I never know what to believe. Except to wonder whether or not I should ditch this place."

Well, that was shocking. Liam, not run The Kelpie?

I looked at Sophie, who rolled her eyes. Clearly this was a threat he'd made before.

"I have to get back to the rooms," she said. "Do you need anything more from me?"

Just answers. But looking at the dancing ghost, I didn't think we were going to get anything else that day.

"No. We probably all need to get back to our lives."

I had a few more clues to add to the scattered information swirling in my head. I still wasn't sure why Delta had thought it was such an emergency, when the flapper ghost had barely talked.

I couldn't help but feel there was a lot going on here that I wasn't being told. The flapper ghost was clearly upset, but something had kept her from telling me the whole story.

And why was that?

Liam and Sophie were already at the door. The teens were staring at me, waiting.

This whole situation was uncanny. And something about the ghost's story...a missing piece of information hovered, then landed.

There were two people in town with a classic trench coat. Chip Lancaster. And Tetris.

Who had recently closed up shop.

"Delta? Do you know anything else? Something you want to tell us?"

She snorted, busily trying to stuff the gnome back

inside her canvas tote bag. "Why would you think such a thing?"

Why would I? She was the one who had called us here. And she'd been friends with Tetris for as long as I'd known him.

"Delta... do you know why Tetris's shop is closed?"

She scowled and scuffed her feet. "Why would I? Tetris doesn't tell me everything."

Maybe not. Or maybe so. But I wasn't going to pry anything from between her pinched lips. Not today, at least.

14

————

After the weird stint at The Kelpie, Stefon and I had gone for a much-needed jog on the beach, then spent the rest of the evening curled up on his couch. Now it was a new, glorious spring day, and I was back at the shop.

Duncan wasn't due in until later and, much as I wanted to be investigating, I had to admit that The Widening Gyre needed my attention.

The shop was still barely making a profit, even with the uptick in tourists now that the weather was fine.

"What do you think, Rhiannon? Can I use you in advertising?"

That would be pretty cute, actually. A black cat and a stack of books. I'd have to ask the teens about it.

Rhiannon blinked her green eyes at me from her perch on the edge of the long counter. She sat, black tail tucked neatly around her paws, next to the display of fancy journals and fountain pens.

Then she yawned and looked toward the front

window, clearly trying to decide whether it was worth the effort to leap down, walk five feet, and leap up again just to chase a patch of sunlight.

She hunkered down into a settled crouch.

"Lazy," I said, leaning over to scratch her head.

I should be going over the accounts, as usual. I hadn't finished them because of the whole teens-bursting-in thing. Or, speaking of, I should be looking over the social media accounts the teens had set up. They'd also updated the store's website and were just waiting on my approval to "launch a social media content marketing campaign."

"Who *are* these girls, anyway?" When I was in high school, marketing campaigns were the last thing on my mind.

A thump came from the back of the store, and since The Widening Gyre had been empty for the past twenty minutes, that could only mean one thing....

"What's up, Biff?" I asked the air, before skirting around the wood counter and pattering down the center aisle, past fiction new releases on my left and politics and history on my right.

The thump came from the paranormal and occult section. Biff's favorite part of the store.

The teens shared his enthusiasm. And they were equally enthusiastic about Biff, whom they really wanted me to use as a selling point to bring more customers into the store.

So far I'd resisted, though looking at the bank balance, I might not hold out for much longer. Especially since I was now paying the teens as consultants.

Bookcases towered along the back wall, with

reading nooks set at each end, and an old-fashioned step stool placed near the central aisle for easy access.

A book lay face up near the cozy chair and lamp set up at the back corner.

"What did you find for me?"

Throwing books was Biff's favored form of communication. He'd owned the shop for decades before my parents took it over and I didn't blame him for sticking around. I'd probably die here, too. And hopefully I'd wait until I was as old as Biff had been before shuffling off the mortal coil.

I reached down for the shiny, plastic-protected book. The cover was blue and white with a pattern of swirls in which fanciful faery creatures swam, strode, and flew.

Unexplained Mysteries of the Faery Kind.

The book was quite the tome, and rested heavily in my hands.

"How many unexplained mysteries of the faery kind are there?" I asked Biff. Not that I knew exactly where he was, but I had a sense of something disturbing the space next to the chair.

The hairs stood up on my neck. "Biff? Did you just move?"

I listened, making sure I was really alone in the store. There were strings playing. A favorite group of mine—Black Violin—whom Stefon had dragged me to see in Portland the year before. A small thump. Must be Rhiannon.

Sure enough, the cat came padding down the aisle not long after, meowing at me.

"Come to investigate?"

As soon as the words left my mouth, the book jerked in my hands, the cover flew open, and the pages flipped frantically.

I yelped, and barely held onto the heavy thing.

The pages moved fast, creating enough of a breeze to whip my hair around my face. And that's no small feat. My hair is long, dark, wavy, and almost as heavy as the book.

Finally, the pages stopped, around three quarters through.

I looked at the page.

There was an image of a pixie, riding a centaur.

And that was the last thing I remembered before Rhiannon and I were both sucked through and into the book.

Or what I assumed was the book.

I looked around. The landscape was surreal. Golden sun shone through pink and purple clouds. Silver birds chirped from ochre trees. I turned. Behind me, Rhiannon stared at a babbling brook.

I mean, it was literally babbling.

The water was streaked with tints of green, red-brown, and purple, just like the marbled end pages of a rare book. It rolled and splashed over rocks and stones, humming, and singing a string of nonsense words.

In English.

"Merry, Humphrey, Faery, Foo. Wizards laughing. Primal goo."

Well, the words made a strange sort of sense, I suppose, arranged in some sort of Lewis Carroll-esque rhyme.

"What do you think, Rhiannon?"

She turned her head, green eyes wide, and mouth open. I could see her sharp incisors and the pink rasp of her tongue.

I'd never seen a cat look aghast before. I was also pretty sure my own face looked the same.

"Aren't you a large, comely, morsel?"

The voice had a low, contralto timbre. I whirled, but saw nothing.

Except...were those faces poking out from between the trees? And what sorts of trees were those, anyway? They looked a bit like cherry and apple trees. And maybe maple. But their leaves were unrecognizable, and their colors, of course, were like no trees on human earth.

"Who are you?" I asked. "Who is speaking?"

One of the large trees rustled round, multicolored leaves. Its trunk was massive, as big as three Stefon's chests put together.

What can I say? I'm very familiar with the measurements of all my lover's chests, past and present.

But wait...I blinked. Tried to focus my eyes. The trunk. Of the tree. Which was moving. As in, not swaying side to side in strong wind—because no storm was big enough to move that trunk without snapping off the whole top of the tree—but actually moving.

Like one of Tolkien's ents.

"Oh. My. Goddess."

The tree stopped. "My name is Uli. And you are?"

"Umm. Sarah."

"It is a pleasure to make your acquaintance Umserrah."

"What is this place?" I asked, not bothering to correct the maybe-ent person. Uli.

"Home," Uli replied. "The place between all places. The well of magic. The sorcerer's dream."

None of Uli's words made a darn bit of sense, so I let them slide.

And then I smelled it, over the strange mix of not-quite-pine, not-apple, not-rose.

Horse.

And trotting through the tree-people came the black centaur, with pixies swirling around her head.

"What are you doing here, human? You were not invited to this place."

Her voice was as cold as the Pacific Ocean in February. I froze, but did not speak.

"The human is fine, Serafina," Uli began. "All magical beings are welcome here and by the smell of her, she has magic in her skin and bones."

"It is not fine. She is a meddlesome creature. And meddlesome creatures get hurt."

Centaurs sure were cranky. At least around me.

"Oh good, the Justice is here. Shall you help us, then?" One of the pixies hovered near me, expectant look on its tiny face.

"How can I help?" I asked.

"The witch must leave," the centaur replied. "She will draw the humans too close to this sequestered place."

"*Sarah!*" a voice called out my name, half familiar, but as if whoever it was shouted through layers of honey.

Before I could turn to figure out where the voice

was coming from, the centaur charged. I felt a pain in my right shoulder.

The pixies shrieked.

Uli shouted. "Noooooo."

And I was screaming, too. "Noooooo!" My voice echoed the big tree's as I hurtled through the blue and purple air.

15

I came to, face mashed onto the carpet runner in the back aisle of The Widening Gyre. I blinked at the dust bunnies crouching beneath the bookcases. Dang. I needed a better vacuum, didn't I?

"Sarah! Are you okay?" That was Tabitha's voice.

But she hadn't been the one to call me.

Then I smelled the Bay Rum and frankincense of Uncle Cyrus.

Rolling onto my side, I spat out a piece of carpet fuzz and slowly sat up.

My head pounded and my throat felt as if I'd swallowed half the sand at the foot of the cliffs. Rhiannon blinked her green eyes at me. She seemed perfectly fine. Stinker.

"Tea," I croaked out. It was the answer to everything, wasn't it?

"On it," Tracy said. Both the teens scrambled off toward the small office kitchen.

Cyrus, handsome as always in crisp, dark jeans and

a neatly pressed violet dress shirt, helped me up and got me settled into the chair at the end of the aisle.

He picked up the book I'd dropped face down on the carpet. Some of the pages looked bent. I winced.

He shook the book at me. "You mind telling me what in Hecate's name is going on?"

I was in the middle of brushing more carpet fuzz off my jeans, but my head snapped up at his tone.

"Excuse me?"

He smoothed the pages of the book and snapped it shut again.

"The teens called me, frantic, mere seconds after I felt you flare and disappear from our realm."

"Flare and...?" Wait a minute. "Did you put a tracker on me?"

I was sore, scared, and suddenly pissed off.

"Of course not!" he said, but he looked away, the light above us shining off the polished, elegant dome of his head.

"Uncle Cyrus..."

I heard the rattle of porcelain on a tray and smelled the distinctive scent of my most expensive oolong. That was not emergency tea, that was sip-and-enjoy tea. As a matter of fact, I should just bring it home.

I kept it in the shop because it was Dad's favorite, for when he felt like celebrating.

And that was often.

"It's important to celebrate the small things," he always said. *"You never know how much time you have."*

My heart lifted, then sank, at the memory.

"Where do you want this?" Tabitha asked, propping the heavily laden tray on one cocked, jean-clad hip.

Tracy hovered just behind her friend, four mugs dangling from her fingers. She looked nervous and seemed to be scanning the air between Cyrus and me.

I didn't blame her. The space was thick with my annoyance and his guilt.

"In the nook under the window." I sighed. "Thanks. I'm going to wash my hands. Be right back."

I threw a *don't think this is over* scowl at Uncle Cyrus, who had schooled his face back into its usual unflappable warlockness, and resisted giving the scowl a tiny magical push in his direction.

Just to make sure he felt it.

Shaking my head, I wound my way through the dark cases filled with brightly colored book spines, toward the break room slash office. Rhiannon followed, then dodged through the half open door to the break room. She probably needed water the way I needed tea.

I continued to the pocket-sized washroom one door over. The mirror above the chipped white porcelain sink showed that I looked spooked. My round cheeks were paler than usual, and I had carpet fuzz on the front of my shirt, as if I'd been grinding my breasts against a carpet creature.

"Great. Just great," I muttered, swiping at the red and blue threads. I finally gave up, washed my hands, and splashed cold water on my face.

"Time to face the strange, uncanny music," I said to the air, as I dried my hands.

The tea should be steeped by now, at least, so that was something.

Nothing like a good cup of tea to cure what ails a witch.

"So, where did you go?" Tracy couldn't hold it in any longer, while Tabitha calmly poured out the golden, fragrant tea into mismatched mugs.

Tracy tugged at her blond hair, while Tabitha simply gave me a small smile and handed me a black mug with the white silhouette of a raven saying "Quote me." Cyrus got the Gashlycrumb Tinies huddled beneath Death's umbrella, and the two teens got Alice in Wonderland characters.

Why was Tracy—who we now knew was coming into the witchy powers she inherited from her mother, Carol—so jittery, and so-far-magicless-though-Wiccan Tabitha so calm?

I would have thought it would be the other way around.

"What happened with the book?" Uncle Cyrus asked.

I blew across the surface of the tea, watching the ripples and inhaling the scent. "Biff threw it, and when I started reading the page it was open to, I...was sucked in. Rhiannon, too."

Rhiannon walked by, sniffed, then headed to the front of the shop. She was clearly uninterested in the conversation.

"Sucked in to where?" Tabitha still seemed too calm, but I took a breath, shook the thought away, and tried to answer.

"I'm not sure. The trees were really strange. And they talked. And"—I turned to Cyrus—"the black centaur was there. The one we met. The tree person called her Serafina, by the way. And she wasn't happy. She charged at me."

"She attacked you?" He sat perfectly still, awaiting my answer, one leg crossed over the other, cufflinks winking in the light, mug wrapped in his elegant dark fingers.

Thinking back, I replayed the scene in my head.

"That's just it. I'm not sure. It seemed like it. She ran at me, but before I could even figure out what was going on, you pulled me back."

He tapped a finger to his lips, and looked over my head at the bookcases behind me.

I don't think he saw the books, though.

16

———

Cyrus left, clearly troubled, and I needed a break to clear my head. I shook the teens off to do more research, or homework, or play video games. Or to go eat ice cream and plot how they would take over the world. You know, the usual stuff teens do. Duncan came in for his shift, thank all the Gods and Goddesses, and rather than work on the books or look over Tracy's and Tabitha's social media proposals the way I should have been, I took my size sixteen self out for a run.

A quick text to Stefon, and he said he'd meet me above our favorite stretch of beach.

I stood at the edge of the parking lot, stretching my hamstrings, and gazing down at the bright, flapping kites, the fallen giants of the trees washed up to shore, and the people.

Unlike the winter beach, where walkers and joggers were few and far between, and families and children were tucked inside drinking hot chocolate, the sunny, springtime beach was filled with activity.

Rain could still blow in at any moment, but the sand would be slightly warmer, and I liked it when noise and laughter flowed back in on the tide.

"Hey, babe."

Stefon's voice warmed me, as usual. I turned to grin at my knight in sweatpants, his favorite Sisko is My Captain T-shirt, and sneakers. The dark, tight curls on his head looked ragged, as if he'd been tugging at the edges, thinking, and his beard needed a trim.

He was gorgeous, anyway.

I rocked on my new minimalist running shoes. They were a gift from Stefon after he got tired of me freezing my feet on winter sand. What can I say? Barefoot running is the only kind I enjoy.

He pulled back, gave me a warm kiss, then scanned my face. "Your text was a bit freaky. You okay after all that?"

I shrugged, a breeze whipping my hair into my face. Digging in the pockets of my sweatpants, I pulled out a hairband and stepped further back to deal with my long, brown mane.

"You know, life of a witch."

"But it's troubling, right?"

Nodding, I looked out at seagulls circling and squawking over something further down the beach, toward the small river that trickled in a shining ribbon across the sand.

I opened my arms, and he walked into them. I wrapped myself around his waist and against the broad span of his chest.

"Not only is it troubling, but I'm starting to think

there are multiple suspects, which means I don't know a dang thing about who killed the pixie, or why."

He placed a hand on my shoulder, and I turned back to look up into his rich, dark eyes.

"And I still don't quite believe that opera singer just had a sudden heart attack. The whole thing feels wrong."

"Let's run. It'll help you think. Then we can get cleaned up, eat something...."

"And then?" I arched an eyebrow suggestively.

He laughed. "Always that. But before then? I think you should use your mother's crystal ball or something. Get more intel. See what you can see."

He headed for the steep stairway set into the cliff face as I stared at his back, and yes, that magnificent butt of his.

But I barely saw them. My mother's crystal ball? I'd used it only once before, and that time?

I'd seen the woman who had been sent to test me.

The one who—it had turned out—had probably killed my mother.

I headed down the long flight of stairs. When my feet hit the sand, I let out a big huff of relief. Stefon wound his way through the fallen giants, and past the taut angles of the long cords that tethered the snapping kites to earth. Children shrieked at the water's edge, hunting for the tiny crabs that burrowed in the wet sand.

I hoped their adult guardians had warned them to avoid the wee jellyfish that also dotted the coastline, as I narrowly avoided two small, glistening orbs myself.

Stefon set an easy pace on a smooth stretch of

damp sand, right where the beach sloped down toward the water. We headed north, loping toward where the fancy hotel—and Uncle Cyrus's favorite local restaurant—tucked itself into the lee of the cliffs, before the dark rock face jutted out towards sea.

The river snaked its silver way to the rolling ocean.

My thoughts snaked and rolled in answer.

The ghosts had seen a trench coat, which meant I needed to pay Seashell Cove's obnoxious reporter a visit. But what in the world did he have to do with the pixie's death? And if he had done the deed, why was he hot on the heels of a story?

Misdirection? Some journalistic sleight of hand?

And what about Tetris? I considered him a friend, but how well did I actually know him?

And as for the centaurs, I just didn't know enough about magical politics to have the first clue what might be going on there.

Uncle Cyrus had been on me about studying, but dang it, I had a barely-squeaking-by business to keep afloat, a life to live, and a handsome man jogging at my side.

"Figure it out yet?" Stefon asked, grinning down at me. The jerk was barely winded. I had really let my cardio lapse lately.

"I don't know what you're talking about." I grinned back, then puffed out an exhalation.

"I can see the wheels turning up there," he said. "If you want to brainstorm, I'm here. That is, if you have the breath for it."

I smacked his arm and huffed out again. I'd been taught to never consciously inhale while running.

Instead, every fourth footfall, I would exhale. The steady pump of arms and legs naturally filled my lungs again. It was a much easier way to run than the hated jogging I used to do in junior high. And sports bra technology had improved since then, too, which was a good thing.

My bosom, as Stefon's friends say in the Society for Medieval Anachronism, is ample. Like the rest of me.

"I've got two possible suspects right now, but none of it makes sense."

A seagull swooped, and we both ducked. Despite the obstacles, running with salt air in my face was one of my favorite things to do.

"I've got a reporter, and a centaur, and a bunch of ghosts. I've got a dead pixie, plus a dead opera singer, which may or may not be related."

Plus, I'd been sucked into an alternate universe with a babbling brook and sentient trees.

"And?"

"None of it adds up."

"Then let it go for now. Race you."

I slowed down for a moment, irritated at being told to let it go. How could I?

But Stefon was probably right. I needed to give my subconscious time to work things out on its own.

I put on a burst of speed, racing past logs and driftwood sculptures and another clutch of flapping kites.

But even the subconscious needs a boost sometimes. I was going to have to start asking some more questions around town.

17

———

After Stefon and I cleaned up, we were both hungry. I'd also had a text from Uncle Cyrus, wanting to meet up for dinner. He wanted to eat at his usual fancy-pants place on the water, but Stefon and I were both in the mood for tamales.

Besides, I wanted to question the chaneques who took care of the gardens outside the Vargas family's restaurant.

If anyone knew about pixies, they would.

I sighed as Stefon pulled into the parking lot.

"You okay there, babe?"

I scanned Main Street. The Widening Gyre was next door, Tetris's fossil shop and Angie's cafe down the way. The daylight was fading, lighting up the banners and flags as the sun dropped west, over the ocean.

Maybe we should have taken Uncle Cyrus up on his offer for dinner on the water.

But there was just too much to do, and I needed carbs and fat to do it.

Maybe even a margarita.

"There's just so much we don't know, and too many people and beings I need to question."

He reached across the seat and slid a warm, enormous hand over mine.

"You've got help, as usual, babe. The teens are on research, the Vargases will help...and surely Cyrus knows something. Right?"

I shook my head. "I don't know. I'm in over my head."

Which was a strange thing to say, considering that the last case had involved someone actively trying to kill me. This one should have felt like a piece of cake, except that I didn't have a plate, or a fork, or even a napkin.

Gah. I dropped the tortured metaphor and got out of the car.

The scent of freshly made tortillas mingled with the salty air, and my stomach rumbled in reply.

We walked around to the entrance, which was past the courtyard on the other side of the building from the parking lot. I looked toward the garden, a pleasant place filled with native plants placed around spiral walkways. A large rock cairn with tiny plants growing in the crevices took up one corner of the garden.

That was the entryway to the chaneque's underground home. I peered through the shadowy cracks past the plants, but didn't see any of the stocky, flat-faced beings.

Stefon was already at the door of the tamale shop, waiting for me.

Patient guy, which was one of his selling points. Unless you crossed him, then watch out.

I grinned. Stefon's quick protection of all who mattered to him—including strangers he considered vulnerable—was another selling point. Yeah. Dating a medieval gamer geek knight made me feel better about the current uncertainties in my world.

There was one safe harbor for me. All I had to do was ask.

He smiled back at me and opened the door with a slight bow, waving me through.

I paused to kiss his cheek.

"What's that for?"

"Because you're you."

He squeezed my hip as I walked into the bright, fragrant restaurant.

Terra-cotta tiles covered the floors and the tables all sported different colored bright serapes sandwiched beneath their glass tops. Uncle Cyrus sat at a table near one of the big windows facing Main, chatting with Davíd Vargas, who wore a red apron over jeans and a white dress shirt. His feet were stuffed into slick basketball shoes, as usual. Among his other qualities, Davíd was a bit of a sneaker head.

Davíd was a longtime friend, and helped his mother run the place. His dad owned Seashell Cove's premier gardening service. Mr. Vargas was as talented with plants as Davíd and Mrs. Vargas were with people and food, respectively.

Davíd rose to hug me and Stefon both. I leaned over to give Uncle Cyrus a sideways squeeze.

Even when he annoyed me, I loved him.

Cyrus had been friends with my parents and was my honorary uncle from the day I was born, a Goddess Father, if you like.

He was also my magical mentor and the warlock who kept me on track.

And that was a pain in the butt. Even though Cyrus had my best interests in mind, I sometimes suspected that his first loyalty was to the Witches and Warlocks Super Secret Society. My name for them, of course. He never told me if the conclave he answered to even had a name.

By the way, the difference between witch, warlock, magician, or sorcerer has nothing to do with a person's gender. It has to do with the flavor of the magic added to a person's natural abilities and training. Sorcerers love the astral planes, witches work mostly with the basic primal elements, and warlocks? Well, I'm a bit jealous of them, actually. Warlocks have super-cool abilities to shift time and space, coupled with affinity for the natural elements. And magicians love high ritual, the kind I really can't be bothered with, so more power to them.

At any rate, I'm a witch like both of my parents, and Uncle Cyrus is a warlock. And we were both dedicated to balancing the magical scales of justice, though I was still getting used to that part.

"Can I get you anything besides menus?" David asked, after we chatted for a moment.

"A margarita, rocks?" I asked.

Stefon asked for a Negro Modelo.

"I'll take a margarita, too."

I arched an eyebrow at Uncle Cyrus. The only

spirits I ever saw him drink were gin and tonics at the height of summer.

He raised an eyebrow back, as if to say, *You can't expect me to drink the wine in this place.*

I took his point. Uncle Cyrus was a major snob. The restaurant's wine list probably consisted of a box of red or a box of white. Or, if you wanted an upgrade, a ten-dollar bottle of either shade, marked up to five bucks a glass.

"Did you meet with the teens?" he asked, once David had headed off to get our drinks.

"Not yet. They're excited about doing research on that book I got sucked through, though. Trying to figure out where it's a portal to, and why. Do you have any ideas about that?"

Cyrus looked out the window. He was as out of place in Seashell Cove as a flamingo, and that was part of what I loved about him. I might never be as snappy a dresser as he was, but appreciated his fastidiousness.

Even if I liked to rib him about it, a family tradition inherited from my parents.

Now that they had both crossed over, it was up to me to uphold all facets of their legacy, including annoying my uncle.

"I've been thinking on it," he said.

Stefon and I both reached for freshly made tortilla chips and tomatillo salsa.

Stefon bumped my hand. I bumped back.

He ceded the chip bowl. Nothing gets between me and food after a run.

It's not that I don't enjoy salads, but warm chips are something else.

Uncle Cyrus watched us, the expression on his face warring between bemused and far away.

"And?" I asked, after I'd swallowed the tangy, crunchy goodness down.

"On one hand, it makes sense you'd get pulled into a book, given your background and current occupation. As a matter of fact, we should look into bibliomancy and other book-related forms of magic. You might have undiscovered strengths there."

I rolled my eyes. Despite having passed my tests—aka The Ordeal—he couldn't let go of teaching me.

David dropped off our drinks, refilled our waters, then wisely left again after we all thanked him.

"Cyrus," Stefon said, "you know I respect the hell out of you, man. But can you please finish your sentence? We need to know what's up."

The two men exchanged one of those looks, where they communicated far more than either of them was willing to say.

Uncle Cyrus took a sip of margarita.

"You are right. I'm stalling. I'm stalling because first of all, books pulling witches into alternate universes is not something I've dealt with before, and frankly, Sarah, it concerns me."

"And?" I repeated, not willing to let him head off on another training tangent. I could feel the need to school me building up inside his aura like a force field.

He sighed. "And why in the world would a centaur want to kill a pixie? There is no obvious answer. The species have always had a symbiotic relationship, that is, when they live in proximity with one another, the way they do here."

Our food arrived, and we thanked the server, a perky young woman with blue hair. She was new. I'd have to ask David about her later.

I dug into the red sauce–smothered chicken tamales and beans. Mrs. Vargas had sent out small side salads, too, which I appreciated, but I needed protein first.

"I feel a 'but' coming on," Stefon said.

"But the centaurs are hiding something," Uncle Cyrus said. "Whether it is related to the murder or murders, I don't yet know."

He picked up his fork, and turned it in his hand, as if it held answers to the questions of the universe.

Then he looked straight at me. I paused, mid-chew.

"And not knowing what they're up to bothers me."

It bothered me, too.

18

———————

Stefon had gaming night at his apartment, and Uncle Cyrus seemed disinclined to talk more, plus, he had the whole almost-two-hour-drive home to the outskirts of Portland, so we went our separate ways.

Why Cyrus didn't just buy a beachside condo in Seashell Cove was a mystery. I mean, why live in Portland, Oregon, if all you had to do was wiggle your nose —metaphorically, of course—and pop into Paris or New York for art, culture, and fine dining?

He had his reasons, he just wasn't sharing them with me.

At least I knew why he drove to Seashell Cove from Portland: he preferred to have a car while he was here.

I puttered around the bungalow as Rhiannon slept on a cushion next to the cold fireplace. She was as much of an enigma as my uncle. Mostly, she lived at The Widening Gyre, but often insisted on coming home with me, mostly during the cold, dark, winter months. The bookshop didn't have a fireplace, after all.

"You're lucky I decided to run by the store to pick up the latest Devon Monk and Nora Roberts books," I said, en route to the bedroom from the tiny laundry area in the scary basement. My arms were full of clean, lavender-scented clothing. "Otherwise, you'd have been stuck at the store."

The black, curled form remained motionless, other than a flick of an ear that told me she'd heard me quite well, thank you, but was ignoring me.

Cats. There was no fathoming their inscrutable ways.

Making my way down the narrow hallway, the thought crossed my mind that the walls were pretty dingy. The whole bungalow needed attention. Paint, for sure. Making the laundry room less harrowing, double sure.

But I realized all of a sudden that it was time to make the place feel more like mine.

"It's not that I don't love you both," I said as I entered my bedroom, "but you're gone from this plane now, and I've got to live my life, you know?"

The air around me shimmered, and I gasped, dropping the laundry on the neatly made bed. "Mom? Dad?"

There was no answer, and no ghosts materialized. Just a faint, sparkling glow, letting me know someone was there, and paying attention.

Rhiannon hopped onto the bed and went directly for the laundry pile.

"Gah! Make some noise, would you? And get off of those. They're clean!"

She blinked her green eyes at me, sniffed, and then

turned. Still sunk into on the laundry pile, she stared at the handmade wood box on my dresser top.

The wood gleamed tonight, as though I'd polished it.

I hadn't.

That was where the glow came from. I stepped closer.

The box was definitely glowing. Clearly, folding laundry was going to need to wait.

I stood, frozen in the middle of my bedroom, not seeing the dirty cream paint or the crack growing up near the right corner of the ceiling. Not seeing the wood trim, the photo of Mom and Dad smiling on the shore, or the scattered mementos on the dresser top surrounding the box.

Mom's crystal ball was glowing inside the box. As far as I knew, it had never done that before, but what did I really know? The thing had sat buried in the closet in Dad's old room for I don't know how long.

I'd only used it one time, and hadn't much liked it. Oh, sure, I'd been thinking I should consult the thing about this case, but that was theoretical. And something I'd meant to discuss with Uncle Cyrus.

Damn it.

Rhiannon leapt onto my shoulder, batting at a long tendril of my hair.

"Hey! You're heavy! And what the heck are you doing?"

I felt her crouch, brace herself...

"Claws, damn it!"

...and spring onto the dresser. The glow of the box

reflected off her black fur as she began to paw at the latch.

"Okay, okay. I get it. Message received."

But it still took me way too long to span the few feet from where I was standing to the dresser, and what I was now thinking of as The Box.

A low humming noise mixed with the sound of bells filled the air. Was the box singing?

And the phone tucked in my rear jeans pocket began to blare and buzz.

That combination meant only one thing.

Trouble.

And sure enough, seconds later, Uncle Cyrus stood in my bedroom, phone held to his ear.

I yelped and Rhiannon hissed. The glowing, buzzing, and chiming didn't stop, however, and my phone was still going bonkers.

"Turn it off!" I said.

He clicked the off button and glared at me.

"What are you doing?"

"Me? I'm not doing anything? The crystal ball is..."

"Why did you take so long to answer the alert?"

What was he talking about?

"You didn't even give me a chance to answer the phone!"

He sliced his hand down, as if to cut off my words.

"Not the phone! That!"

One long, elegant finger festooned with a heavy silver ring pointed toward the now-vibrating wood box.

"Wait. What? The crystal ball is a phone?"

Rhiannon glared at me, and Uncle Cyrus threw up his hands.

"Just. Open. It," he ground out.

My palms were sweating and I wiped them on my jeans. Tucked my hair behind my ears.

Took a step forward.

Then a second step.

Rhiannon scootched away from the box, which was rocking and shaking by this time.

"Oh, for Goddess's sake!" Uncle Cyrus exploded. "You're a Justice! Do what is necessary."

I whirled on him. "And who was the one who was supposed to train me? Why didn't you ever tell me about the box?"

Rhiannon began to yowl.

I'd had it. I bumped up against the dresser, flicked the small latch, and opened the box. The crystal ball floated, bobbing softly up out of its velvet cradle, until it hovered, suspended, just above the top of the box.

It was beautiful. Shimmering. Humming. Chiming.

It sang to me. It sang my name.

In my mother's voice.

I burst into tears, and through the liquid haze, reached out my hands and grasped the crystal orb.

It was warm to the touch. Comforting.

And then, just as suddenly as all the noise and strangeness began, it stopped.

I took in a shuddering breath, and clasped the heavy orb to my breastbone.

In the sudden hush, the only sounds were my ragged sobs and Rhiannon's rumbling purr.

Uncle Cyrus cleared his throat.

"I apologize. You're right. I didn't tell you. And I should have."

Then his arms were around me, and I was breathing in the scent of frankincense and Bay Rum.

"But I really need you to pick up whatever message the orb is trying to send through."

"Can I at least blow my nose?" I asked, pulling away from him. "And can we talk about this first?"

I knew I was stalling—and so did Cyrus and Rhiannon—but so what?

Rhiannon leapt from the dresser and walked out of the room.

"You do that," my uncle said, patting my shoulder. "I'll put the kettle on."

Cyrus followed the cat.

I just stood there, still clutching the smooth orb. It was calm and inert again, but felt as if it was waiting.

Clearly, there was way more to being a witch—and a Justice—than anyone had bothered to tell me.

Questions swirled inside my brain as I stood, blinking from the laundry pile on my neatly made bed, to the dresser, and the photo of my parents.

Carefully, gently, I placed the crystal ball back inside the velvet-lined wooden box. It gave one soft chime before I closed the lid.

My mother's crystal wasn't done with me, but I just couldn't deal right now.

Because of all the questions I had, the one rising rapidly to the top?

Shook me to my core.

19

After blowing my nose and splashing cool water I my face, I joined Cyrus and Rhiannon in the living room, that question still rattling my brain.

"Is my mother's spirit trapped inside the crystal ball?"

I held the box, cradled in my arms, its sharp corners digging into my arms, helping to ground me again. The thought that she might have been stuck in a box and shoved into the back of a closet made me feel ill.

Uncle Cyrus looked as smooth and unruffled as if nothing had happened, in his usual dark jeans and a spring-colored, flowered shirt. He set the tea things out on my coffee table and slid gracefully into one of the wingback chairs.

This was another room that needed freshening and redecorating.

But where was I going to get the time or money for it?

I sighed and sat down on the couch across from

him, setting the box on the coffee table next to the fat Brown Betty teapot.

"The answer to your question isn't as simple as you might think."

He sat back in the chair and crossed an ankle over his knees. His jeans rode up slightly, revealing teal socks with a navy lattice pattern. The blue-green harmonized with his shirt, of course, and his Italian leather shoes looked soft as butter, with the dull shine of polish.

"So, spell it out for me as if I was, oh, I don't know, a magical apprentice who needed training and information, even though I'm now supposed to be a full-fledged witch."

His calm, thoughtful gaze only annoyed me more.

"You are correct. I should have trained you in all of this, but..."

"But what, Uncle Cyrus? I thought your super-secret super-powerful group had systems and protocols and all the rest. Why in all the nine worlds do I feel like I'm half trained and facing down a dragon with a stick?"

"You remind me so much of her. Him, too."

My rising anger dropped like a stone into a cold tide pool. I sat, hands gripping my thighs, willing myself to remain still. To wait for him to finish.

The box gave off another chime and we both looked at it. Rhiannon jumped onto the couch and sat next to me, staring at the box as if it were some sort of magical mousehole.

The box didn't do anything else, so I looked back at Cyrus. His eyes looked sad.

"You still haven't answered my question." I said the words as gently as I could. He just kept staring at the box, not speaking.

Giving him some time, I leaned forward to pour the now-oversteeped tea. Oh well, I'd just add some extra milk to mine.

Slightly bitter with tannins, the brew was still comforting, and just what I needed, despite it being well past eight p.m. and not the time I usually drank caffeine.

Uncle Cyrus shook himself and reached for his own mug. Not bothering to doctor it, he took a sip, grimaced, then added a bit of sugar and stirred.

The click of spoon against mug seemed loud to me, and the air felt thick.

Thick with decades of unspoken words.

"I hope it's just the residue of your mother's magic in the ball."

I swallowed, carefully. "But you aren't sure."

"No." The word was choked out, as if his throat was closing in, clutching at the truth.

"Cyrus. What the heck? Can't you find out? Do something?" There was heat in my words, but I thought I was doing pretty well to not be ripping my hair out and shrieking like a harpy.

"I didn't know..." he whispered. Dang. This must be bad. Cyrus was always confident. Uncle Cyrus always had the answers, or at least acted like he did.

The orb chimed again, louder this time, and the box buzzed.

Rhiannon placed one paw on the lid and it calmed down. But I had a feeling that was very temporary.

"So...this part of the conversation isn't over. You owe me a full explanation, but for now, tell me about this alert system. What do I need to know?"

He set his mug down on the low table and looked up at me, eyes still sad, but with a flash of gratitude mixed in.

Then he leaned back in his chair, crossed an ankle over his knee again. Shot his cuffs. Regained his Uncle Cyrus-ness.

"Here's what you need to do..."

20

It had been a late night, working with Uncle Cyrus, and I needed one of Angie's blueberry muffins and a large cup of English Breakfast tea.

Desperately.

Pot of tea steeping quietly in front of me, I sat at one of the rear tables of the Blueberry Café, watching the morning bustle and blinking my tired eyes. Angie's café was a pleasant place, filled with blond wood tables, and cheerful art for sale on the bright white walls.

Besides, it always smelled like my idea of heaven, if witches had a heaven. Which we don't. But if we did? Yeah, it would smell like the Blueberry Café .

All the window tables were full of people enjoying the spring sunshine, strong cups of coffee, and Angie's specialty baked goods. There were some locals I recognized, including Delta Crabbit, who hadn't seen me yet. I should have greeted her, but by the time I noticed she was at a table across the room, I'd already sat down and was not inclined to go anywhere.

My body was sore from the beach run, and my brain was sore from Uncle Cyrus's poking and prodding, and my vain attempts to figure out what the heck was going on with the crystal ball.

Yeah. We'd worked into the wee hours, and I still didn't know what the thing was trying to tell me.

I watched as Delta broke off a piece of double chocolate muffin, looked around, and sneaked it to the seat next to her. It looked as if she was feeding her tote bag.

Must be the gnome, trying to stay incognito.

Looking past the windows out to Main Street, I realized I hadn't been to visit Tetris in a while. Last time I'd been by, the fossil shop was closed. I got it, given that he was his only employee, sometimes stuff happened and he had to close.

But I hadn't seen him around town at all.

Not since the pixie died....

And the fact that he sometimes wore a battered old trench coat like Chip Lancaster's? Still bugged me.

But what bugged me more was the fact that I might need to suspect a friend.

Angie stood next to my table, blond hair tucked into a blue kerchief, apron smeared with a streak of chocolate. She plunked a white plate on my table, set a cup of coffee down, and sank into the other chair with a groan.

"I can't stay long, but I could use a quick break."

"Busy morning?" I asked out of politeness, before stuffing a big bite of warm muffin into my mouth. Oh. My. Goddess.

"You have no idea. I feel like I've been running since I got up at four."

"I'm glad you're a baker, Angie," I said, once I'd swallowed. "But I'm equally glad I'm not."

The sounds of the cafe continued as we both sat in silence for a moment, me enjoying the uh-maze-ing muffin, and Angie sipping her coffee.

With half the muffin safely inside my stomach, I picked up my tea.

"Have you seen Tetris lately?" I asked. "Last time I went by his store, it was closed."

Angie rubbed her nose. "You know, I haven't. Last time he was in was a week ago."

Just before the opera singer and pixie were found dead.

"What's the frown about?" she asked. "You worried about him or something?"

Angie had been part of solving the magical problems we'd had over the winter. She'd started out a suspect, but I'd quickly realized she'd been a tangential victim of the dryad killer.

At some point, I needed to ask Uncle Cyrus about how much I could talk about this stuff to people. But until I did...

"You heard about the opera singer? At The Historic Kelpie?"

Angie nodded.

I leaned across the table and lowered my voice. Angie leaned in to meet me.

"A pixie died at the same time. In The Kelpie's garden."

"Liam must have freaked!"

"Oh, he did. And Delta was there, too."

Angie and I both turned to look across the café.

Delta turned, too, and was staring at us.

Caught.

I waved, and then motioned her over.

She scowled but fussed with her tote bag and started over.

As she wound her way through the cafe tables, tote bag swinging perilously, the café door opened, and the bright pink head of my best friend and former girl-friend, Cecilia, looked around, spotted us, and forced her own way through the crush.

"I've been looking all over for you!" she huffed.

I looked at my phone. Sure enough. Five missed texts.

"Sorry. What's wrong? I haven't seen you in days!"

She waved an impatient hand at me, just as Delta and her gnome-filled tote bag arrived. "Toby says you need to come. They found something in our garden."

At the same moment, my phone and Delta's both set up a buzzing racket.

I checked my texts and looked at the older witch. "Somethings gone wrong at the inn."

"Ghosts in an uproar," she nodded grimly.

I looked from Cecilia, who was tapping her purple Converse All Stars in impatience, to Delta, and to the gnome, who by this time had popped his head up from the tote.

"What should we do?" I asked.

I was the official Justice, but Delta had decades more experience.

"I'll take care of the inn," the older witch said. "You go with her."

She jerked a chin at Cecilia.

I nodded, grabbed my cross-body bag, and bent to clear my dishes.

Angie waved me away. "Just go."

Cecilia was already halfway to the door. I followed her pink head.

"Uncle Cyrus," I muttered, "I hope you're available."

Because whatever was going on? I had a feeling it would take a village to help.

21

———

Cecilia struggled with the lock on the wooden door to the old 1960s era home she shared with her partner, Toby the hob.

I paused at the threshold to remove my shoes.

"Come on! No time!" she called over her shoulder as she raced past the living room and down the white hallway hung with fabulous art.

Things must be serious. Cecilia always removed her shoes.

As I loped after her, bag thumping against my hip, a strange sound echoed down the hall. It was coming from the kitchen and sounded like a combination of buzzing tattoo needles and seagulls shrieking.

I burst into the bright kitchen space.

Toby was huddled on the floor, their petite body pressed against the cabinet beneath the white porcelain sink. The window above them was open, red-striped curtains flapping.

Bright colors whirred and swooped through the air,

flashing in the sunlight and reflecting rainbow arcs all over the white kitchen and Cecilia's collection of vintage red, green, blue, and yellow kitchenware, which was somehow still nestled safely in its pride-of-place spots on the live-edge wood shelves.

The rest of the kitchen? Was a mess.

Flour spread across butcher block counters and the black and white floor tiles. Honey dripped from the small table in the nook near the back door.

The white powder coated Toby's dark brown hair and brown jeans, mixed with what looked like chocolate syrup and strawberry jam.

Cecilia crouched next to Toby, stroking their dark hair.

"What is going on?" I shouted over the din of shrieks and what I now knew were not tattoo needles, but wings.

Dozens of pixie wings.

I stood frozen in the kitchen doorway. How had Cecilia even gotten through the shimmering, buzzing phalanx of angry-sounding creatures?

Think, Sarah. What would Cyrus do?

And speaking of which. "Uncle Cyrus, you can show up anytime, here!" I threw the thought out as I spoke the words. He was always popping in when I didn't want to see him, and now?

Nowhere. Just me and a frightened hob, a frantic friend, and a bunch of pissed-off pixies. At least, they sounded pissed off, and as far as I knew, didn't usually trash people's kitchens.

Start with the basics, Sarah. You're here to help. Luckily, my inner voice was smarter than the rest of me. Right. I closed my eyes for a moment, to shut out the whirring fury. Then, inhaling slowly, I sent an energy cord down into the earth beneath the house. Reaching below the basement, the pipes, and the disturbed layer of earth, down to where things were calm. Stable.

I drew on that sense of stability to calm and center myself. Then I called on my psychic awareness and opened my eyes again.

And saw that the pixies were crying.

That was so not what I expected, but at least it gave me a starting point.

"How can we help you?" I asked.

The frenetic, angry buzzing slowed. A few pixies alighted on the backs of the chairs set around the small Formica table in the center of the kitchen space.

I waited, completely still, keeping my breathing slow and even, and my magic contained.

Toby's sniffles and Cecilia's comforting murmurs were finally audible. While I wasn't sure what had caused the hob such emotional distress, I was certain the state of their kitchen wasn't helping matters.

Hobs could not abide a mess.

"How can we help you?" I repeated. "Can you tell us what is wrong?"

A pixie with golden-brown skin and green wings as iridescent as a beetle's back scowled at me from dark brown, red-rimmed eyes.

"One of our comrades is dead, and this *hob* desecrated their grave!"

Toby looked at me, eyes still streaming with tears.

"I was just taking out the compost. I didn't even see the grave."

"You did!" shrieked a golden-winged pixie with milk-pale skin and green eyes. "And you stepped right on it!"

Toby started to speak again, but I held up a hand.

"Show me the grave. I am a Justice and need to make a reading of the situation before coming to a verdict."

No need to mention I was new to the job and didn't have much experience with pixie burial rites. If it would keep Toby's kitchen from further damage and buy me more time, I was going to rely on whatever tools I had.

A little stalling for time never hurt anyone, did it?

The first pixie sniffed. "Very well. Follow us."

In a blur, the creature sped out the window.

I realized I had no idea what pronouns pixies used for themselves. Toby was a they, but I didn't think all hobs were. And the pixies all looked similar, and were of an indeterminate gender to my untrained witch's eyes.

As the rest of the pixies streamed out the open window, Cecilia helped Toby up from the floor. I followed them to the kitchen door and out into the neat, lovely garden.

It was a proper kitchen garden, with pots of herbs on a small back porch, and raised beds of vegetables. In one corner stood a venerable apple tree, and in the corner opposite, the bright flutter of pixie wings drew my eye to a large, black, compost bin tucked next to a blue lobelia bush.

I continued toward the bright flutter, as Cecilia and Toby paused on the porch so Toby could fuss with the herb pots. It seemed like a strange thing to pause for, but then, I'm not a hob.

The scent of roses and lavender mingled with the soft tang of salt air. I wished this was just a pleasant spring afternoon and I was sitting with my best friend and her partner, drinking lemonade and enjoying life.

But, needs must.

As I crossed toward the pixies, I realized Uncle Cyrus still wasn't here. It was unlike him to not answer two calls in a row, especially when he was so close by.

My brow creased in worry. I hoped it didn't mean something worse was on the horizon.

The pixies parted as I approached, and I saw a small cairn of pebbles on one end of a small depression in the earth.

I wrinkled my nose as the scent of composting kitchen and yard scraps hit me.

"Why on earth did you bury your friend here?"

Oops. Hadn't meant to blurt that out.

"Rowena asked the gnomes to dig the hole and we didn't realize where they'd dug it until it was done," said the golden-winged pixie.

I could see why Toby had stepped on the grave. "So, it seems pretty clear to me that Toby is telling the truth and that it was an accident."

The hob stepped up next to me.

"May I, Rowena?" the hob asked the beetle-green-winged pixie.

The pixie, now perched on a weathered cedar fence post, nodded.

Toby stepped forward, then bent to place a bundle of rosemary and pink roses on the little grave.

"I do apologize," they said. "And please know that I will tend to your friend's grave for as long as I live here."

"Oh," said the golden-winged creature, "there is no need to tend it that long. Tamina will be long gone by then."

Toby looked as confused as I felt.

"A pixie's spirit only lasts as long as their body remains," said a purple-winged sprite. "One moon cycle."

Toby nodded.

"So," I said to the assembly, "if this problem is laid to rest, shall we head back to the porch, and you can tell me about these deaths?"

Luckily, the sprites agreed that the porch between the house and Toby's herb garden would be a pleasant place for a meeting, because my nose couldn't take the compost bin anymore.

22

———

Cecilia went inside to get some lemonade, and Toby followed her, probably to start cleaning up.

As the pixies gathered, I checked my phone for messages, hoping Delta would have contacted me with news.

Nothing.

What could have both ghosts and pixies so agitated?

Cecilia came out with a pitcher of pale-yellow liquid, and Toby followed, a tray of glasses rattling in their hands. Toby's face and hair were damp. The hob had cleaned themself up, along with starting in on the kitchen.

The golden-winged pixie hovered near my head, which was distracting, but I wasn't sure what would insult them, and the pixies were already so agitated, I swallowed my irritation and looked to the one with the beetle-green wings.

Rowena, Toby had called her. She definitely seemed in charge.

Toby had set small glasses of lemonade on the porch rail and handed me a larger glass. I smiled in thanks, then turned my attention to Rowena.

"One sprite has died, that we know of, and two others disappeared," she said.

"Do you know what killed them?" Cecilia asked. Her pink hair shone in the sun, reminding me of how beautiful she was. We'd settled into a comfortable friendship once the lover part of our relationship was done, but I swear, sometimes I was reminded of why I'd been attracted to her in the first place. It was mostly just who she was, but she was gorgeous, too.

The pixies all looked at Toby.

"Herbs," the golden-winged one said, having finally settled on the porch rail next to a lemonade glass. "Dangerous herbs."

We all looked at the hob, who looked at the porch boards, clearly uncomfortable.

"I keep a few small pots in the kitchen, near the window. Things like thyme are good for humans and hobs, for cooking, but I know they are dangerous to some other magical beings."

"But who would want to hurt the sprites?" I asked. "And would the same thing have killed the opera singer?"

The garden gate squeaked, and around the side of the cottage walked Uncle Cyrus, dark, shaved head gleaming as if polished. His eyes looked grave.

"It would kill a person if it was mixed with

foxglove," he said. "Or lobelia. Or even valerian in the right dosage."

Toby's already pale face blanched. "I have all of those in the garden."

"What do you know?" I asked Cyrus.

Uncle Cyrus stepped up onto the porch, the pixies making way as if he had communicated something with them. For all I knew, he had. Uncle Cyrus should have looked out of place in this semi-wild, Oregon coast cottage garden, but he looked right at home. He always looked right at home, despite his polish. I tried to blend in, but stuck out like a curvy, size-sixteen thumb wherever I went.

What can I say? Tall women don't blend in too well.

I narrowed my eyes at Cyrus. Upscale Black men with shaved heads and silver jewelry should stick out, too. He had to be using a glamour.

"The autopsy report came in." Cyrus said, leaning casually against a section of porch railing not covered with sprites. He looked at me. "We've got a contact at the coroner's office."

"And?" Toby said.

"It was a heart attack, as first thought, but there was digitalis—foxglove—in her system, along with other trace herbs that the coroner didn't know to look for, but our person did."

"Did you notice any herbs at the scene?" Cecilia asked.

I shook my head. "No. But I wasn't looking for them, either."

I felt foolish about it, too. I really needed to get

better at this Justice business if I was going to be of any help to the community.

The last case, and now this one, were proving to me that no one person could mete out justice on their own.

It takes a village, and all that. Or a kooky seaside town.

"I've got to get over there," Toby said. "Who will come with me?"

Several pixies fluttered forward to answer the hob's call, and Cecilia took her lover's hand. That was good.

"Good thing I'm on staycation, huh?" Toby sent Cecilia a rueful glance. "I have time to help investigate a murder."

"It's not what we wanted," Cecilia agreed. "But we had a few days together, at least."

Then my best friend turned to me.

"Let's go."

23

———

Uncle Cyrus rode with me. The Fiat was a bit small for both of us, but he'd long ago stopped complaining. So what if no one but skinny teenagers would fit in the back seat, and all I could carry were a couple of sacks of groceries? What more did a witch need?

Especially when she had a boyfriend with an SUV and a trailer built to haul medieval camping gear?

"Delta is at the inn, checking in with the ghosts," I said.

Uncle Cyrus turned from the window to look my way. I spared him a glance, then put my eyes back on the road. The Historic Kelpie was coming right up, and I needed to navigate the turn.

"Do the ghosts have more information for us?"

"I'm not sure yet. Our phones buzzed at the same time, and then we split up. I haven't heard from Delta since."

Or the gnome. Maybe he could help Toby and the garden pixies.

Delta and the gnome sat out on the little iron landing at the top of the back stairs. Delta's white hair was sticking out, as if she'd run a scrub brush through it, and the gnome's purple cap was askew.

"I don't think you should come up here," Delta called down as Uncle Cyrus and I approached by way of the courtyard that skirted the inn.

"Why not?"

The gnome poked his head between the iron pickets. "The ghosts are in a snit."

"We'll come down."

Delta's sneakers smacked against the iron steps, creating a ringing melody given counterpoint by the rhythmic thump of the gnome leaping from step to step with both boots at once.

It really would have been faster and easier for us to climb upward, but I'd learned the hard way that there's really no arguing with Delta Crabbit. Or most witches, come to think of it.

Finally, they both reached the ground, the gnome's apple cheeks red with effort.

"What's wrong?" I asked.

"What isn't wrong?" Delta replied, jerking her head toward some metal chairs and café tables on the patio outside The Kelpie's dining room.

I looked at Uncle Cyrus, who shrugged and followed the older witch, making way for the gnome to pass ahead. The rumble of a V8 engine and the slamming of heavy doors announced the arrival of Toby and Cecilia. They joined us, followed by three of the pixies.

Once we were seated, with the pixies perched on the apple branches overhead, I looked at Delta again. She'd tried to smooth out her shaggy white hair, but only succeeded in making it stick out in different, more interesting ways. She looked like a deranged cockatoo.

"Why don't they make these chairs taller?" the gnome grumbled. He stood on one of the chairs, chubby pale fists braced against the iron table.

"I could get a booster seat from inside," I offered. "Or a cushion."

The gnome just glared at me. I'd thought I was being helpful, but clearly, I'd hit a nerve. Stepped in it somehow.

This whole case felt a bit that way. Too many angles, too many facets, too many ways to screw up.

"The ghosts wanted to know why you hadn't been back to talk with them," Delta said, staring at me accusingly.

"Why didn't you, Sarah?" said Rowena, fluttering her beetle-green wings. She sounded more sad, than accusing.

"I'm sorry! I've been a little busy chasing after centaurs, getting sucked into weird realms, being threatened, and trying to keep the store from going bankrupt!"

"Sarah. Why didn't you tell me things were so dire?"

Uncle Cyrus's voice was gentle, and that made my throat tight. I looked out at the tall fir and cyprus trees, the apple tree, and the low, hardy bushes. A whimsical sculpture of flying sprites rotated slowly, creaking, in the light breeze.

"It's not actually that bad." I sighed. Well, maybe

things were that bad, but I didn't want to get into my woes in front of all these people. "But I still don't get it, Delta. What exactly do the ghosts want from me?"

"The daft fools pooled what brains they have left among all their automated sequences and remembered some other things," the gnome interjected.

I frowned. What did gnomes know about automated...?

"What?" he asked, rosebud mouth turned down into a frown.

"Sorry. Nothing. You just sounded like Stefon there, for a moment. What did they come up with? And why didn't you want me to go in?"

"They've worked themselves into a lather over what they feel is your shoddy treatment of them."

I inhaled, about to protest, and Delta held up a hand.

"You asked. And you are going to need to talk with them soon, but I'd give them some time to calm back down."

Uncle Cyrus huffed, clearly wanting to get on with things now that he was here to help.

"What exactly is this vital information you have, Sarah?" he asked.

"The ghosts think the singer was murdered. And the pixie tried to stop it." Delta said.

"And what about the person in the trench coat?" Cecilia asked.

"You need to ask Liam about that," Delta replied.

24

———

"All right, that's it." I smacked my hands on the table, wincing as my fingers hit the hard iron. As I pushed myself up, the others scrambled, confused, to follow. I stomped across the courtyard—not easy to do in sneakers—and flung open the doors to the dining room of the inn.

Barely noticing the paneled walls and strange, seafaring artwork, I stomped across the battered oak floors to the kitchen and slammed the door open. Empty. Whirling, I almost crashed into Delta and the gnome, who was riding on her shoulder. Uncle Cyrus stood in the middle of the dining room, arms crossed over his chest, one eyebrow raised in question.

"Where are Toby and Cecilia? And the pixies?"

"They went to the garden to see if there are any traces of herbs to find." Cyrus's voice was smooth and calm, which only highlighted my own annoyed state. Was that what I was supposed to aspire to, now that I was a full-fledged witch? Calm in the face of dumb-founding adversity?

Well, I wasn't there yet.

I scowled and stomped off through the bar, toward the lobby, following the scent of popcorn and the sound of voices.

One of the voices sounded a lot like Joan Fontaine, which told me that the ancient television above the equally ancient popcorn machine was playing old movies again. But Joan Fontaine's wasn't the only voice I heard. There were also two men talking, as I stepped out into the lobby with its overstuffed velvet couches and all the horror movie posters, and the rideable shark visible through the window. Liam looked up, startled, and the other person yelped and ran up the stairs, trailing popcorn as they went.

"Oh no you don't, Tetris!" I raced after the old punk-rock fossil dealer and tackled him on the stairs. Popcorn flew everywhere, bouncing off my face and tangling in my brown hair.

"Oh, what do you have to do that for?" he grunted.

"Where have you been?"

We both staggered upright. I brushed popcorn off the shelf of my chest and flipped crumbs from where I'd crushed them against my knees of my jeans.

"Why were you running?" I asked. I had so many questions for him. Too many questions. "And where is your trench coat?"

"What?" Tetris looked genuinely confused. "My trench coat is in my room, upstairs."

We entered the upstairs parlor, the beautiful Art Deco space filled with Chesterfield sofas, well-stuffed chairs, an electric fireplace, and tons of books and strange nautical paintings. Tetris slumped down on one of the overstuffed sofas, raising a light cloud of dust. I heard the others coming up the stairs, with Liam muttering about not grinding the popcorn into the carpet. I didn't blame him. But I also didn't have time to deal.

Good thing Toby was in the garden, or the hob might be tempted to clean up the inn.

"What are you doing here? Why is the shop closed?" I asked again. Tetris sighed and looked across the room at a portrait of an old sea captain who had his arm around a mermaid. Come to think of it, the mermaid looked a little bit like me. That was creepy.

"You wouldn't understand," he said.

"No, you don't." It was my turn to cross my arms over my chest. "Try me."

He looked at me, eyes rimmed with red. Sometimes his eyes were red because, you know, he smokes a fair amount of pot. But I didn't think that was the case this time. He'd been crying.

"Tetris? What's wrong?"

"I loved her," he choked out, then burst into sobs, slumping over his knees, head in his arms. Delta sat down next to him and tentatively patted his knee. The gnome perched on the sofa arm.

"There, there," she said. "It's going to be okay."

He snorted, then dragged a well-used hankie from his jeans. "How do you know? How do any of you know? It's not going to be okay. She's gone!"

Duh. I was a little slow, wasn't I? It finally dawned on me....

"You're talking about the singer?"

"Who else would I be talking about?"

"But I don't understand... And why did you disappear? Why are you staying here?"

Liam cleared his throat from where he leaned against the wall. "He just needed some time out, so I offered him a place to stay."

"This was her last place. I just needed to be near where she was."

Well, that explained why she came all the way down to Seashell Cove to record a record when she could've gone to Portland. Or used the studio at her own university.

I didn't want to, but I had to ask.

"Did you kill her?"

Tetris's head snapped back as if I slapped him.

"How can you say that?"

I regretted the words as soon as they had left my mouth.

"Sorry, I had to ask. I had to rule you out."

"Why would you even think...?"

"Your trench coat," Delta said.

"The ghosts saw someone with a trench coat leaving..." I chimed in.

::*That's right, we did,*:: said a new voice. I looked over towards the wall across the room and there, hovering in midair as though standing on a staircase, was the flapper from the speakeasy upstairs.

Oh my gosh. This was weird even for me. Nothing to do but roll with it, though.

"What did you say?" Liam asked, completely unruffled by her appearance. I guessed that, running The Kelpie, he had to be used to it.

::*I told you,*:: she said, tapping one T-strap shoe on a step that didn't exist, before walking all the rest of the way down, swishing her handkerchief hem. The rhinestones and feathers on her fascinator dimly flashed in the weak light filtering through the windows.

It made me wonder if ghosts could become more or less substantial as they wished. I glanced at Uncle Cyrus. I had way too much to learn.

::*I saw the pixie,*:: she said, ::*and a flash of something, and later I saw someone in a trench coat running away.*:: She leveled her eyes at Tetris as she said that.

He choked back another sob.

"I didn't do anything," he said. "We had a date, and I dropped her off. We were talking in the garden... Then she said she needed to get inside to rest because she had a recording session first thing in the morning. If I had known something bad would happen, I would've stayed. But I saw Sophie cleaning inside the dining room, and thought she would be safe. How was she not safe?"

He collapsed again, sobbing into his knees, fingers running through his gray hair.

And then I noticed, for the first time, he wore solid black, down to his usually colorful Doc Marten's. He was a man in mourning.

I hoped that meant I could strike him off the suspect list.

"Tetris?" I kept my voice as soft and comforting as I could. Delta shot me a look, but I shrugged. If we waited until he pulled himself together, we'd get nowhere, fast.

"Did you see anything strange before you left? Or as you were walking home?" Because that was where the ghost had to see him going. He lived up the hill from The Historic Kelpie.

He tilted his head up, but stayed curled in on himself. "Like what?"

"Like, I don't know, a centaur?"

Fear flashed across his face, but was just as quickly gone, replaced by confusion.

"What are you talking about? I've never seen a centaur. Everyone knows they don't come into town."

Yeah. Everyone knew that, except that one had.

And Tetris was afraid of something. If he just "needed space," he would have closed the shop and stayed at home.

He was hiding at The Kelpie for a reason. Now I just needed to figure out why.

25

U ncle Cyrus, Stefon, and I were back at the Vargas's restaurant, sitting at a glass-topped table with a turquoise serape beneath the glass. Much as I wanted a margarita, I had forgone alcohol for agua de Jamaica instead. The hibiscus drink was slightly tart and sweet. Delicious.

Uncle Cyrus followed suit, though Stefon went with Mexican Coke, and Stefon and I were making short work of the basket of fresh, warm tortilla chips and green tomatillo salsa while Cyrus stared out the windows. I could tell he didn't see what was in front of him, but was looking at something far away.

"Should I have pushed Tetris some more?" I asked, before shoving another loaded chip in my mouth. Next to me I felt Stefon shrug.

"He wouldn't have told you anyway. Probably better if he doesn't know you're suspicious."

"Uncle Cyrus?" Cyrus gave a slight jerk and his dark eyes snapped back into focus. He took a sip of his own hibiscus drink before answering. "I think Stefon is right. Tetris is wrapped up in himself right now, and it's best if he stays that way. The last thing we need is him interfering."

David came up and delivered three plates of tamales, house-made pickled peppers, salads, beans, and rice.

I looked up at my friend, who needed a fresh red apron. He looked as if he'd been battling with carnitas in the back.

"Do you have a moment to sit?"

He wiped his hands on his apron and looked around the restaurant before nodding and pulling out a chair. "Any luck today?"

That was a question, wasn't it? I felt more confused than ever despite all the work we'd done.

"Not really," I replied, cutting off a bite of gooey tamale with the edge of my fork. "We did figure out more pixies have died, though, and we think there might be poison involved. Toby and some pixies checked out The Kelpie's garden and found traces of some herbs that shouldn't have been there. Have you heard anything from the chaneques?"

"Poison herbs..." David wiped a palm across his face. "That's bad. Nasty."

I had to agree.

"The chaneques say that something bad is in the soil, but they can't seem to tell me what it is."

"The soil?" Uncle Cyrus's head snapped towards David, eyes as intense as a hawk's. "What do they mean by the soil?"

David shook his head. "Like I said, they haven't

been able to explain it in a way that I understand. But my dad says something's up. He's noticed the plants seem off—that's how he puts it—like spring is delayed or something."

I sat back, the tamales forgotten for a moment. "Why would anyone want to delay spring? And, like, isn't spring already well underway?"

No one answered, but I didn't really expect them to. I turned to Uncle Cyrus. "Do you think the centaurs have something to do with this? Is this what they're hiding?"

He shook his head. "I don't know." His face looked very troubled.

Stefon cleared his throat, then took a swallow of his Mexican Coke before setting the chipped glass bottle down on the tabletop.

"Let's go through all this again," he said. "One, something's wrong with the soil. Two, at least three pixies that we know of are dead. Three, there's a dead opera singer. Four, the ghosts are agitated by something and saw someone in a trench coat. Five, Tetris is hiding something. Six, what am I missing?"

"That's a lot of variables, but I have to get back to the kitchen." David, said scooching his chair back and standing. "Let me know if you come up with something or if you have any more questions. I can talk to my dad again, see what he says."

"Thanks, man," Stefon said.

"Yeah, thanks, David," I echoed.

Uncle Cyrus just gave him a nod and David hoofed off to the kitchen where I knew Mrs. Vargas was cooking up a storm, the way she always was. Especially when she was stressed.

We ate in silence for a while, all of us thinking. Finally, I had stuffed as much food in my head as I could, and shoved my plate away, groaning.

"You always eat too much here," Stefon said, grinning before shoving another forkful of food into his own mouth.

"It's not my fault Mrs. Vargas's cooking is so good." I patted my stomach. "What are we missing? There's something about the pixies and the centaurs, something about poison in the soil... I still don't see what the opera singer has to do with anything."

"You never did consult the crystal ball, did you?" Uncle Cyrus asked.

"Holy Mother," I said, "you're right. You and I got to talking and it stopped pinging at me, and I just forgot."

Cyrus looked thoughtful. "Did you forget, or did something *want* you to forget?"

"Who could do that?" Stefon asked, aghast. He was quite a trooper, my boyfriend. He'd gone from not really knowing about magic to just rolling with all sorts of weird stuff.

Cyrus pursed his lips as if he was fighting back a harsh truth that he wasn't sure I was ready to hear.

"Cyrus?"

Stefon grew very still and said his fork down, sitting up straight and placing both feet firmly on the floor as if he might have to fight someone. My knight in shining armor, even in a taqueria on the Oregon coast. I was glad he had my back.

"I have my suspicions," Uncle Cyrus said, "but I'm

just not sure. I really think we need to go consult your mother's crystal ball."

"I suppose you'd want to do that right about now," I said.

"I'm kicking myself, Sarah," he said. "I should've made you do it the other night when I was at your house."

"Why didn't you?" Stefon asked, pulling out his wallet, getting ready to head to the cash register.

"Because something made me forget to."

Suddenly, despite the warmth of the restaurant, and my belly full of warm food, I felt chilled as if it were January again.

26

———

S tefon was on warrior knight duty at the door. But unlike the last time we did this magical operation, the living room wasn't full of people, and the fireplace was cold.

I also felt less certain about using Mother's crystal ball this time. I knew more about what the tool could do and wasn't sure I was up for it.

But the community was trying to figure out these murders, and I was part of that, whether I was acting as Justice, or as just an ordinary witch.

So, I sat on the couch in the living room I still needed to redecorate, filled with my parents' memories. And my mother's crystal ball sat on its silver base on the coffee table, flanked by two candles.

Maybe this was what it meant to be a Justice. It meant following the lead of the people who needed you most.

That was comforting somehow. Following the lead of the people meant I didn't make the rules. It also meant I wasn't the one who had to go dashing off, flailing a sword around, hoping I hit the right target.

It meant I could leave the sword wielding to Stefon, who actually knew how to use one. It meant I could leave the bulk of the research to the teenagers, who loved that. And I could listen to the counsel of the chaneques and the pixies, the Vargas family, the hobs and gnomes, and all the rest. Even the centaurs, though they seemed to be hiding something rather than helping.

I looked at Uncle Cyrus, who sat in one of the chairs across the coffee table from me. His handsome face was placid, and he looked completely cool, calm, and centered, the way he almost always did. The jerk. Maybe I would be that way someday too, though I doubted it.

"Okay," I said. "I guess I should get this party started, huh?"

He raised one eyebrow, but said nothing, so I shrugged, and began my centering protocol. I slowed my breathing down and made sure my feet were flat on the ground, and my spine was floating up from my pelvis, just the way I was taught.

"Let me see what must be seen. Let me hear the silent sound. Let the truth in center form, from light and dark, spellbound." The magical phrase was more for my own mind than a call to anything outside of me, but magic operates on several levels, you know? So, whether anyone besides myself and Uncle Cyrus was listening, and whether the smooth hunk of crystal on the coffee table heard?

It didn't matter. What mattered was the ritual.

Ritual trains the witch's heart and mind, the teaching goes. Theory is, that ritual helps the rational mind shut up for a minute so other skills and talents can move to the forefront. Kind of the way a writer does best if she prepares a cup of tea first, or the way an artist needs a certain kind of music. It's all ritual, opening access to deeper...

Cyrus cleared his throat. Yeah. I was stalling. And now I needed to start over.

Reciting the cantrip inside my head this time, I lit a candle, the flame hissing as the match hovered next to the wick. I picked up the candle on the other side of the crystal ball and touched its wick to the flame until it caught, flaring, and then settling into a steady glow as I placed it back in the brass holder.

Inhaling deeply again, I did my best to return to my center and soften my vision. Soft focus was a thing I'd always struggled with. It was the ability to look at something without fully focusing on it, and it was one of the basic tools in a witch's toolbox. My breathing deepened, and I kept my eyes steered toward the crystal ball on the coffee table, allowing the candle flames to dance at the edges of my vision.

My mother's crystal was partially cloudy, partially clear, and shot through with cracks and striations that traced interesting patterns inside the orb.

"Show me," I whispered. "Show me what I need to know."

And the filing system in my mind flipped through a cascade of images and sounds. The centaur's hoofbeats. The pixies, wings flickering in the sun. Tetris. The gnome. Delta's scowl. The dancing ghosts with their papery cologne scent. The images flickered like the candle flames, moving past me one by one, as though my fingers actually flipped through a physical filing cabinet.

And suddenly, a vision opened, not in my mind, but deep within the orb.

The scene was at night, focused on a milk-white centaur with hair as pale as proverbial moonlight. Surrounded by shadows, it knelt on its front legs at the base of the cypress tree. Hands covered his face, and his broad shoulders shook.

The centaur was sobbing, repeating words I could not hear.

I tensed. Straining to hear.

Which was the exact opposite of what I was supposed to be doing.

Inhaling deeply, I softened my edges again, letting my exhalation relax tense muscles and nerves. I fought off the urge to focus, which would chase the vision and the sound away. Slowly, the words became clear.

"I'm so sorry," the centaur said. "This was not supposed to happen. You were only supposed to be the messenger. Oh, ancient Gods, what sorrow!"

I inhaled. Exhaled. My breath skated across the crystal orb and the vision brightened, then grew cloudy...then changed.

I saw Chip, tapping his pencil on the edge of a notebook, pasty face scowling.

I saw the ghosts hovering near a window.

I saw the pixies flittering frantically, perching on bushes, worried looks on their small faces.

I saw two small, delicate-winged shapes plunge toward the earth.

"Show me. Please," I entreated the crystal orb. None of this was making any sense. I needed to see who had done the thing. Who had killed the sprites and the opera singer and who knew what else?

And then I saw her, the ghost I had been talking with. With her speakeasy clothes, and her T-strap shoes, and the feathered fascinator perched on her chiseled bob of hair.

She had something in her hands. It glinted in the lamplight.

It was a glass vial. The liquid inside it looked murky.

"What does it mean?" I whispered.

The ghost's head snapped up, her sharp chin pointed at me. Her eyes looked damp, even through the striations of the crystal *ball.*

::It means that even ghosts can make mistakes.:: The thought was clear as a bell inside my head. *::It means that even ghosts can kill.::*

I shivered, and the candles extinguished themselves, first one, and then the second. All that was left was smoke, spiraling into the air.

27

I heard a ragged sound. It was my own breath, heaving in my chest. My body was covered in a cold, greasy sweat. Nice. I was a witch who needed a shower. But first, I needed answers.

"Did you hear that?" I asked. "What did she mean?"

"Stefon," my uncle called, "close down your wards."

Cyrus leaned toward me, face intent, keen interest dancing in his eyes. "What happened?"

"The ghost..." I heard the swish of Stefon sheathing his sword, and then him, padding back into the living room in his stockinged feet. I felt the couch sink as he sat, his large body displacing the cushions next to me. His warm big hand rested on my thigh.

But I didn't look at him. I kept my eyes on Uncle Cyrus's face, thoughts sifting through the images, trying to figure out what to say. Cyrus was preternaturally still. Waiting.

I exhaled noisily. I wasn't going to form a coherent

narrative, no matter how hard I tried, so I might as well just start talking.

"It was the ghost from the inn. The flapper. She was holding something. A small glass vessel, filled with murky liquid. And she said that even ghosts can kill."

Stefon muttered a mild curse, and Uncle Cyrus sat back in his chair.

He looked off into space, long graceful fingers drumming on the chair's arm. He might as well have been drumming on my breastbone, the way my heart jumped around inside my chest.

"Well." Uncle Cyrus blinked. "I've heard of such things, but I didn't actually believe they were possible."

"Thought exactly what was possible?" Stefon asked.

"I've heard that ghosts can move physical objects sometimes," Uncle Cyrus said.

"Like in *Poltergeist*?" Stefon's love for geeky old films was ever-present.

Uncle Cyrus and I both shook our heads.

"No," I said. "Poltergeists come from psychic phenomena, made by living humans. Telekinesis. Usually kids hitting puberty. Cyrus is talking about something else. Something I've never heard of at all."

Cyrus tapped a finger on his lips and shifted in his chair once more, crossing and uncrossing his perfectly pressed jeans, bright slivers of socks flashing beneath the crisp denim hems.

It was strange to see him so discomforted. I guess this was another part of my becoming a full-fledged witch, and a Justice. A new phase in my adulthood. Maybe that was what the Saturn return everyone blathered about really signified. It was about becoming fully an adult with all its implications, including realizing you're it. You might get help solving your problems, but no one was going to make them go away.

"It might be something to get the teens on," Cyrus said. "Doing some in-depth research on the topic. Meanwhile, though, I'll see what I can figure out via my own resources...and my memories."

I was growing tired, losing energy with this we-have-no-answers conversation. "Can you tell us anything right now?"

"I can tell you this is much worse than we feared. If the ghosts of The Historic Kelpie killed someone, I'm not sure what we're going to do."

"Meanwhile," I replied, "we still have other people on the suspect list."

We all looked at each other, and paused.

"But none of us believe it was any of those people, do we?" Stefon's words hung in the living room air.

Neither Cyrus nor I replied.

We sat in silence for a while, until finally I'd had enough.

"This calls for some wine." I shoved myself up from the couch. Stefon rose, too.

"I'll help."

We entered the kitchen, and he took me into his arms. I gratefully allowed it, resting my head on his broad chest, feeling the solidity and strength of him. It was one of the perks of the relationship: I was finally with someone larger than I was. Sometimes a witch just needs a big body to hold onto, you know?

"You okay?" His voice rumbled in his chest.

"Not really," I replied. "But I don't have much choice right now, do I?"

Sighing, I stepped away from his warmth and opened the fridge, fingers heading unerringly for the opened screw-top bottle of Pinot Grigio in the door.

Stefon got down some glasses. He paused before leaving the kitchen, leaning into me. I tilted my head back for the offered kiss. It was sweet. I needed some sweetness.

Back in the living room, Cyrus was looking out the window, even though dark had fallen.

"Something out there?" Stefon asked, suddenly on alert.

I set the bottle down on the coffee table and grabbed the glasses from Stefon's hands as he went to stand next to Uncle Cyrus.

I looked at them. Two tall, handsome black men in the largely white state of Oregon, both of them so different. Stefon with his tight curls and beard, and Uncle Cyrus with his smooth, shaved dome. Stefon was muscular and bulky where Uncle Cyrus was lean, and Stefon dressed like a geek in jeans and a T-shirt while Uncle Cyrus looked as if he had spent the day shopping in San Francisco.

But they would both fight to the death if it mattered. And they were both important to me. They were both, I realized suddenly, part of my family. That was a change, wasn't it? I'd gone from barely admitting Stefon was my boyfriend to considering him an indispensable part of my life.

"Well?" I asked, pouring myself a glass of the pale, golden liquid. "Is there something out there?"

"There's a centaur." Uncle Cyrus said. "It was hard to tell at first because her hide and skin is black, but I can see her eyes shining, do you see it?"

Stefon peered through the glass and then nodded. "Holy moly, I sure do."

I took a sip of wine and then set the glass back down. I guess I wasn't going to get to drink it after all. "Let's go see what Serafina wants."

As we trooped onto the front porch, I pulled on a sweater. The Oregon coast was cold, sometimes even at the height of summer. And spring was as variable a time as there was possible to be. Solar lights lit the pathway through the rocky garden, and sure enough, down where the pathway met the road, a streetlight gleamed on the sidewalk, and at the very edge of the pool of light was the centaur.

"Oh good," she said, "you heard me."

She danced a bit from hoof to hoof, then seemed to realize it, drawing herself up, standing tall again. But she didn't quite radiate the strong authority she'd had when I'd met her before.

"What business do you have with us, Serafina?" Uncle Cyrus asked. I stood, arms crossed over my chest, wishing I had grabbed a hoodie or a jacket instead of just a cardigan. Live and learn. Still, having been raised on the Oregon coast, you'd think I would know better by now. Or be acclimated to the cold like Stefon seem to be.

"There's trouble," she said.

"No kidding," I muttered, then spoke up. "Really? You came here to tell us that? After you charged at me and kicked me out of wherever that place was?"

Huh. Yeah. I was still a little pissed about that.

"Sarah," Uncle Cyrus said, a note of warning and reproach in his voice.

"I'm sorry, but I feel like we've been jerked around enough. What are you doing here and what does it have to do with the deaths? The murders?"

She actually flinched a little at my words. Well, that was a change, wasn't it?

"I know we have treated you poorly," she said. "We are unused to dealing with non-centaurs. We live in isolation and that is just our way."

"You still haven't told us what you want, though," Stefon said, standing firmly at my side.

"Is there somewhere we can go that is less exposed?" the centaur asked.

I jerked my head. "Come through the side to the backyard. We can talk there."

I didn't wait for a response, but simply skirted my way through the garden towards the side of the house, and on through the wooden gate that needed repainting. There were solar lights back here too, and a slice of ocean that could be seen on clear days through two of the houses behind. Tonight, all I could see was a dim froth of white and hear the crashing of the waves.

The sound of my childhood. The sound that soothed me to sleep. I led the way to a rear corner where some lawn furniture hunched among more solar lights clustered in a half arc. There was a fire pit in the center too, and I was tempted to light it, but I didn't know how long we would be here. And I certainly didn't want to encourage the centaur to stay.

Speaking of which, I noticed none of us sat, preferring to stand even if none of us were as tall as the centaur. At least Stefon came close, and I caught him looking at her, as if assessing whether he could take her in a fight. I didn't want to have to bet on that one.

"Please," Uncle Cyrus said, "tell us what you know."

Serafina pawed at the ground, then raised her head. "Just before the last full moon the pixies came to us for help. They said there was trouble in the gardens beneath the cypress trees, above the ocean cliffs. That is too near to human dwellings for us, so at first we did not listen. We told the pixies they needed to take care of it themselves.

"Just past the full moon they returned, now frantic, and begged us. So finally, we relented, but found it was too late. Our scout found strange herbs scattered and a dead human and a fallen pixie. He placed the little one upon a bush so it would not get trampled, and so its companions could find it. He brought samples of the strange herbs back with him."

"And what were they?" Uncle Cyrus asked.

I shivered and pulled my sweater closer, wishing Toby was here, or the chaneques. Someone who understood more about herbs.

"Some of the flowers that can heal or harm, and even centaurs or pixies know to take care with them. But the others? We had not seen them before."

"So why are you here now?" I asked. "I don't understand. What's changed? What do you want from us?"

28

I was truly baffled, and felt the pressure around my aura that was a signal that we were running out of time.

"We need you to solve this problem," the centaur said. "If something can kill both pixies and humans, perhaps it can kill centaurs, too."

"I don't get it," Stefon said. "How do you know that? And why come to Sarah now?"

"Because the centaurs had a conclave and decided that a thing that can kill both magical beings and those who carry very little magic is a threat to us all. Also..." Serafina turned and stared at me with those eyes that were such a rich dark I could barely see them in the dim light.

"You have been named Justice. And it is up to you to do the work the pixies asked us to do. If this does not get solved soon, we shall move deeper into the woods, and farther from the threat."

"If the threat is magic, you can't escape it, you know." My words felt like arrows in the night.

The centaur jerked and drew herself up, face fierce. "We will do what we must. That is how we have survived for thousands of years. Make no mistake, if something comes for us, we will strike back. And we care not who dies."

Then she simply turned and trotted back toward the garden gate.

"Some of you care," I kept my voice soft, but it carried far enough to make her pause. "One of you was crying as if he felt remorseful. As if the death of at least one of the pixies was his fault. Do you know anything about that?"

Her shoulders tensed and her head jerked, but she didn't turn. My words were a challenge, and she knew it. But she didn't turn back. She simply flicked her fingers, as if dislodging an insect or throwing out a protective ward. Then she shoved her horsey bulk back out the garden gate.

I heard her hoofs ring upon the concrete walkway and heard when she began to gallop upon reaching the tarmac on the street.

"Well," Stefon said beside me, "that was interesting."

I barked out a laugh.

"You can say that again. We have a lot of people to talk to tomorrow, but for now, I really want to finish that glass of wine."

I shuffled through the dark garden in the direction the centaur had gone.

"Um, is there a reason you're not going through the kitchen door?" Stefon's voice came from behind me.

I shrugged and continued through the gate. Truth was, I wasn't sure. Something compelled me. Despite wanting nothing more than to curl up on my couch with my boyfriend, the back of my neck felt itchy. Tingling.

Maybe I just needed to make sure the centaur was really gone, or maybe...

"Hey! What are you doing?" I shouted.

I saw a flash of trench coat and heard an *oof* and the sound of shoes scrabbling through rocks and bushes.

I ran, Stefon right behind me, just as the trench-coated person reached the sidewalk.

"Stefon!"

He barreled past me and within seconds had wrapped his massive arms around a struggling sack of tan coat and began dragging the person back toward me.

It was Chip Lancaster, our intrepid journalist and resident pain in the butt.

Uncle Cyrus came to stand at my side.

"Are you spying on me?" I asked, hands on my hips. I was suddenly awake, and warm with indignation despite the chilly night air.

"Or were you planting something?" Cyrus's voice was dry as snakeskin.

"No! I was just gathering intel! I'm a journalist! The ghosts..."

As if realizing he'd messed up with those last two words, Chip clamped his pasty lips shut.

I took a step forward, closing the gap, but remaining just outside spitting distance.

"The ghosts what?"

He shook his head. Stefon tightened his arms. A streetlight bounced off his flexed muscles and made his beard gleam.

"Let me go! You have no right to detain me."

"You have no right to be skulking around the lady's home in the dark." Stefon kept his voice mild, but I heard the steel underneath. "What do you want me to do with this rat?"

That last was clearly addressed to me. And, much as I wanted that glass of wine, and a shower, and to go over the suspect list with Cyrus and Stefon, and to deal with the rest of this mess in the morning? It wasn't going to happen. That was clear.

"Stuff him in your car, please. I'm going to get my purse and a jacket."

"And then?" Uncle Cyrus asked.

I sighed.

"We're going to the inn. Whatever this is, it stops tonight."

I could practically feel the disturbance wafting out from The Kelpie. The gray, cold, Art Deco miasma of the ghosts swirled in my mind's eye.

Then I felt Delta. She was frantically signaling.

She was signaling me.

"I've gotta go!" I shouted, whipping my head from left to right. Stefon was half dragging, half shoving Chip into the back of Cyrus's car, as Cyrus leaned against the other door, making sure the reporter could not escape.

Or maybe he was just staying out of the way.

"What's taking so long?" I jogged toward the car. Chip was hanging onto the top of the passenger door, streetlights bouncing off his white knuckles.

"This. Fool. Won't. Cooperate!" Stefon grunted.

"Oh, for Goddess's sake! Cyrus! Can't you magic him in?"

Cyrus just grinned, as if enjoying himself.

The pressure built inside me. Magic. Growing.

A strange sound rang and clattered in my ears. I shook my head. The sound resolved into hoofbeats just as Serafina turned the corner of my street and barreled toward me. Majestically, of course.

She pulled up to a stop, barely winded. Looking down at me, she scowled.

"Why are you back?" I asked.

"It pains me to say this, human, but the crisis is severe. Hop on."

I looked at her broad back, naked waist, and ahem, avoided looking at her equally naked chest. Then I glanced at Cyrus, who still wasn't helping Stefon.

Then back at the centaur, who stamped one impatient hoof.

"I don't like this any more than you do, but I think you're right." Guess my purse and jacket were staying behind.

Hoping against hope I would not fall off, I stepped up onto the curb, grasped that muscular waist, and slung one of my thankfully long legs over the centaur's broad, black back.

And held on.

"Lock the house!" I shouted at Uncle Cyrus. "And good luck!"

And then my stomach lurched, and we were off, hooves ringing, as I held on for dear life.

29

———

There was no time to enjoy the ride. No time to panic, either. Turns out a centaur on a mission is fast. Really fast. And my jarred spine and aching thighs made sure I knew they weren't happy with it at all.

Jogging on the beach was clearly not the same as riding centaur-back. I'd be paying for this jaunt, for sure.

Serafina barreled up the back driveway at the historic inn, stopping so quickly I almost catapulted from her back. My torso slammed into her human back and I grabbed on, narrowly missing her...chest.

She turned her head and snapped her teeth at me.

Geez. You'd think she wanted to get rid of me or something. It wasn't as if I'd grabbed her on purpose.

"Get. Off."

I slid to the gravel, sneakers crunching as I landed, hard, jarring my knees. Serafina was big. I'd give her that.

"Thanks for the lift," I said as I paused, one hand

braced on the stair rail to the rear of the building, groaning and panting.

She snorted and trotted toward the courtyard. Running my fingers through my hair, wincing at the tangles, I turned to follow and was stopped by a flash and a pop.

And there was Uncle Cyrus, Stefon, and Chip.

Stefon looked slightly ill, and Chip hung like a rag doll from his arms. The reporter looked as if he was going to puke all over his trench coat.

Uncle Cyrus, of course, looked as if he'd just stepped out to take the air outside of a French chateau or something.

"You can transport other people? Why didn't I know that?"

He shrugged one elegant shoulder beneath his navy blazer.

"I try not to," he said. "It's a bit of a strain and bends the rules. But getting that oaf into the vehicle was proving tiresome."

"You abducted me!" Chip's face was red in the lamplight, and he stood upright again.

"Be quiet," Stefon growled, tightening his grip. The reporter blanched, but didn't say anything more.

"Serafina headed that way. Come on." I'd grill Uncle Cyrus later, when we had some time. I was beginning to regret being a witch with limited abilities to bend space and time to my will. All I could do was alter the configuration of existing elements on the physical or astral plane. Cyrus told me that a warlock's talents weren't that different, and that it was simply a matter of concentrating differently. But he always followed up by trying to explain particle physics, and math, and all sorts of other things that made my eyes glaze over.

So, maybe I'd stick to my electric Fiat after all.

I hurried around the building toward the courtyard, letting Stefon and Uncle Cyrus deal with Chip.

The centaur paced in the courtyard, snorting like a horse, which sounded frankly strange coming from a human nose and chest. No time to think about centaur anatomy. I slammed open the dining room door, then stopped, staring at the chaos that greeted me. Uncle Cyrus bumped into me.

"Sarah? Make way, please?"

I found my feet again, and stepped into the maelstrom.

The dining room was in an uproar. Good thing the death of the opera singer had cleared the paying guests. Liam must have cancelled the bookings he'd had in the main portion of the inn. At least, I hoped he had.

Frankly, I hoped the whole place was empty, despite it being the start of the busy season at the coast. Whatever guests were staying in the annex buildings' family suites that flanked the front courtyard would still have had to notice something strange going on in the main building.

Lights flashed on and off overhead. Behind the kitchen door, cupboards slammed and I heard what sounded like water turning on and off in the metal industrial sink.

Liam sat at the long community table in the center of the dining room, head in his hands, moaning.

Delta hovered near him, white hair sticking out all

over, looking half panicked. I didn't see the gnome anywhere.

"Delta! What's going on?"

"The ghosts have all gone bonkers, and I have no clue how to stop them."

Well, that was pretty obvious. I paused to think, but the noise and fury didn't make it easy. I watched Stefon park Chip on a chair next to Liam, and Delta placed two firm hands on Chip's shoulders when the reporter started to rise.

Stefon began easing toward the kitchen door, and I was about to suggest he not open the damn thing when the swinging door slammed outward, almost clipping his nose. He leapt back and landed in fighting stance.

That's my boy.

Three ghosts came barreling out, two wearing sharp suits and one in a beaded evening frock. I didn't know ghosts could barrel anywhere, but these ones managed somehow. And sure enough, one of the suits carried a stack of plates in its shimmery arms.

"How in the world?" I said.

"What's happening?" Stefon called, his head snapping back and forth, searching for an enemy he clearly couldn't see.

"Three ghosts, one with crockery and one with...duck!"

Stefon ducked and squatted just as a martini glass —thrown by beaded frock lady—flew where his head had been and crashed into a framed painting of a mermaid luring a ship toward a large rock. Glass flew everywhere, narrowly missing the gnome, who'd chosen that moment to enter from the bar.

"Eep!" He squeaked and scrambled back.

"Stop!" I yelled, and raised my hands in what I hoped was an impressive gesture. I called on the wind from the ocean, gathered the energy the ghosts were flinging all around the space, and made a gesture to calm the storm.

At least, that's what I thought I was doing, but considering one of the ghosts raised a plate and hurled it toward my hands, my magic was having the opposite effect.

Great. Just great.

"Uncle Cyrus!"

"I'm working," he muttered.

"Well, work harder!"

I stepped toward the one ghost who wasn't throwing anything. He was a small man in a pinstripe suit with broad lapels and an equally broad tie. His features looked Japanese, which wasn't a particular surprise, though during the 1920s, most Japanese communities were further inland.

"Sarah? What are you doing?" Stefon's voice was tentative. Still in fighter stance, he looked around the room, a determined look on his face, as if he'd wrestle a ghost to the ground if he had to. Even though he still couldn't see them. I filed *what can Stefon perceive or not* away for later conversation.

"I want to talk with this gentleman here." I said the words out loud but also sent the thought to the ghost. If he couldn't hear me on this plane, perhaps he could listen in the æthers. You know, the astral planes where all kinds of stuff is possible. "I bet he knows what's happening. Don't you?"

He smoothed a hand over his slicked-back, heavy hair, and lit a slender cigarette. *::It is none of your affair.::*

"Oh, but it is, you see. Because Liam is my friend, and you are in his place." No need to mention the me-being-Justice thing. Not yet. "So, please tell me, what is going on?"

He looked off into some unseen distance, and I saw the slight adjustment of his shoulders and face that signaled he'd come to a decision. He trained his dark eyes back at me, clearly curious and interested. *::We have a murderer in our midst, and some of my friends are quite unhappy. I tried to tell them that we've had smugglers, bootleggers, gun runners, and thieves among us all along. What, then, is a little murder when we ourselves are dead?::*

Huh. I had to admit, his logic stumped me for a minute.

"I need to talk to your murdering friend. I assume she's still upstairs?"

::How do you know who it is?::

"I'm a witch." Another plate hit the wall. By this time, Delta, Chip, and Liam were crouched, hiding beneath the long table in the center of the room. Stefon had moved beside me. Apparently, I was a safe zone for now. Uncle Cyrus was nowhere to be seen. I was on my own.

::A witch?::

"Yes. A witch." I didn't need to explain myself to this ghost. "Can you please tell your friends to calm down? I'm here to try and fix things."

The martini glass–flinging woman wailed. *::You cannot fix the dead!::* Then she hurled another glass.

Where was she getting all of them? I swear, she wasn't carrying that many before.

"You're right. I cannot fix the dead. But I can sure as heck try my best to help the living. There are pixies, centaurs, and humans who are bereft right now, and I'm going to get to the bottom of it."

I turned back to the Japanese man. "You fix the situation here. I'm heading upstairs."

Which is likely where Cyrus had slipped out to, dang him.

But if the wailing, crockery-hurling spirits down here were any indication? He wasn't having much luck either.

30

———

Three centaurs were in the back garden area, clustered near the outside stairs.

"Something bad is going on here, and I don't like it," Serafina said. The other two centaurs stood slightly apart. I recognized the one with the milk white coat and moonlight-pale hair from the crystal ball. His eyes were red-rimmed, and his arms clutched at his chest as if trying to keep himself from flying apart at the seams. The third centaur kept a steadying hand on his shoulder.

"You need to fix this," Serafina said, fire sparking in her dark eyes. "You're the Justice now."

I huffed out a breath and headed up the metal stairs, Stefon right behind me. He may not be able to see ghosts, but his big presence was comforting.

I opened the door, making sure to step inside this time, giving Stefon room. I fought the urge to turn and head straight back out, down the stairs, and back home.

After the maelstrom downstairs, the speakeasy was...worse.

A big wooden radio sputtered and screeched as the Bakelite knobs jerked between 1930s dance music, static, and news broadcasts. Ghosts brawled on the dance floor, their faded limbs flying through the air, connecting with other ghostly bodies. The smell of old spilled whiskey and gin was almost suffocating. I breathed shallowly, swallowing down a sudden bout of fear and insecurity.

Despite having battled a powerful sorcerer, and having passed my test and all the rest, I felt woefully unequipped to deal with whatever the heck was going on here. Dead pixies and opera singers. Whatever the mystery was with the centaurs.

And ghosts doing things no ghosts should ever do.

They didn't really need me, right? I mean, it was ghost business, right? And Seashell Cove had gotten along just fine after my mother died, and then, when Dad got sick.

Right?

Besides, Cyrus was better trained. Better equipped... Stefon nudged me. "Babe. You've got to do this. But remember, you're not alone."

Warmth filled me at both his words and his touch. He was right. I wasn't alone. I was never alone. Justice was never dealt out by one person.

It took a community. And I was part of that. It went against my oaths to leave it to the ghosts, or even to Uncle Cyrus.

Cyrus stood in the cozy seating area off to the side. Ghosts shimmered and swirled around him. They were in various stages of manifestation. Some looked almost fully present, while others were mere wisps of corporeality.

I exhaled, and walked toward my uncle. The warlock who was more family to me than any blood relatives I might still have. My uncle looked calm, serene almost. I breathed more deeply, fighting not to gag at the spilled booze scent and the ghostly miasma.

"Center yourself, Sarah," I muttered out loud, though I doubted anyone else could hear me with the ruckus going on.

Step by step, I navigated through random ghosts, the soles of my shoes sticking on spilled alcohol. As I grew closer, I realized that Cyrus stood over a sobbing ghost. The flapper with the glass vial.

Her shoulders shook with weeping. The feather fascinator was askew on her bobbed hair.

Her hands clutched at a limp handkerchief. So, where was the vial?

I looked at Uncle Cyrus.

"She was waiting for you," he said. Then I saw he had a small glass vial in his left hand.

"Waiting for me?"

He simply nodded toward the ghost. Okay. Right. Here we go.

And why did it feel easier to battle an angry sorcerer than it did to crouch down next to a distressed shade and ask her what was wrong? But I did it, anyway.

"I'm here," I said. Then I made the mistake of patting her knee. Uh. Don't do that. Don't ever pat any part of a ghost's body. It'll just squick you out. Trust me.

I wiped my hand on my jeans. Yeah. Shower time later. As soon as I was done with whatever this was.

The ghost sniffed, raising her watery eyes my way. She shimmered in and out of focus with every slight, hiccupping sob.

"Can you tell me what happened?" I said, as gently as I could.

::I... I'm not exactly sure. I just wanted her to stay. It's been so long...::

I glanced back at Cyrus. He crossed his arms over his chest, offering no help.

"Wanted who to stay?"

The ghost's face twisted, as if she was in extreme pain. She pointed across the room, to where two armchairs flanked the radio. One of the chairs was occupied by a ghost whose jeans, draped sweater, and thick, long hair that must have been varied shades of brown and silver in life.

The breath whooshed from my lungs as my brain scrambled to put two and two together.

Was that...? Realization dawned. "The singer."

The flapper burst into noisy sobs just as Delta dragged a sweaty Chip Lancaster into the room. Considering that Chip outweighed the older witch, she must have been using a bit of small magic to compel him. Both of them looked around uneasily.

The ghost extended her hand again and shrieked, the noise ricocheting inside my skull. Ouch.

::It was him! He made me do it!::

Our heads all snapped toward the reporter. Alarm flashed across his face and he struggled in Delta's grip, flailing toward the door. Stefon ran to block him.

"I didn't do anything!" Chip shouted. "It was you! You're the one who said you loved her singing! You're the one who wanted the deal with the centaurs!"

So, our intrepid reporter could see ghosts. And knew about the centaurs. Interesting.

But that didn't leave me any closer to solving the...

I snapped my fingers and raised my voice to carry through the din. "Everybody! Stop! Turn off the radio. And stop fighting!"

"Sarah?" Uncle Cyrus asked.

"I think I know what happened."

"Stefon, bring Chip over here, please."

Chip struggled harder. Stefon became an immovable rock, which seemed to be one of his knightly powers. Or something.

"Settle down," Stefon growled, and frog-marched the terrified-looking reporter across the groaning wood floors, Delta walking behind them, one hand extended in case of funny business. Stefon shoved Chip into the chair without the opera singer's ghost in it.

Also interesting. Stefon may not have been able to see the ghost, but he could sure sense her.

I crouched down, and forced Chip to meet my eyes, the distressed flapper hovering near my back. Since that caused an uncomfortable tingle up my spine, I did my best to ignore her, and focus on the flesh and blood human in front of me.

"You wanted a story, didn't you?"

He looked away, eyes fixed on a nonexistent spot on the floor, chewing on a hangnail. "I don't know what you're talking about. You have no right to harass me like this."

Well, that burned. "Harass you? Harass *you*? After all…"

Stefon's hand came down on my shoulder, breaking off my indignant rant. "I got you a chair. Sit."

"Thanks." I huffed out the word, still annoyed, but he was right. This was no time to yell at Chip, satisfying as it might be.

I sat in the slightly musty, upholstered wing chair and tried not to think too hard about the last time it had been cleaned. Out in the courtyard, I heard the centaurs stamping. They must be wondering what the heck was going on.

"You were chasing a story and decided it would be easy to create one, didn't you?"

The opera singer gasped, one pale hand flying to her lips. ::*You used me?*::

::*He used us all,*:: the flapper replied.

Every eye in the room was focused on Chip, who shifted in his chair. Uncle Cyrus moved to stand next to the chair, with Delta flanking the other side. Believe me, Chip noticed. His head darted between the ghosts, and me, and Stefon, and Delta, and Cyrus.

The ghosts moved closer, drawn to our little grouping like moths to a cobwebby porch light. The reporter was trapped.

Chip burst into tears.

31

I forced myself to not roll my eyes. The guy seemed genuinely upset, but for someone who I suspected had not only caused the mess we were in, but then tried to blame it on me?

My sympathy level wasn't at an all-time high.

"A pixie and a human are dead, Chip. And two other pixies are missing. You need to buck up and tell us what the heck happened here."

The flapper moved to stand next to the opera singer, placing a reassuring hand on her shoulder. Both ghosts stared. Waiting.

"You don't know?" His tear-streaked face was blotchy, but hope shone in his eyes.

"Not so fast, bucko. I've got a pretty good idea, but I want to hear it from your lips."

Every witch knows that words have power. If I could get Chip to speak them out loud, it would help me do my job as Justice. His answer would help seal his fate.

And if he lied to me? Well, I might have to call in

human law enforcement, and I wanted to avoid that at all costs. Besides, what would I tell them? *"Oh yes, your honor, our key witnesses are a distraught centaur, some pixies, a hob, and a ghost."*

Yeah. That was so not happening.

::You made me think it was all my fault.:: The flapper had dried her ghostly tears and there was a firm set to her delicate jaw.

The singer just looked sad, and mildly confused. I could well imagine why.

The other ghosts moved even closer. I forced myself to breathe normally, though the atmosphere around the old cabinet radio had grown thick as coastal fog.

The red blotches on Chip's face flared, then he blanched again.

"You're already in trouble, Chip, you may as well tell us your side of the story." I kept my voice calm and steady, reasonable even, which was saying something. I really wanted to throttle the twerp.

A buzzing sound came from the doorway.

"What the heck?" Chip yelped as two pixies dive-bombed his head.

"Cyrus?"

Uncle Cyrus made some motions with his hands, forming a shield around Chip's aura. The pixies bounced off it, buzzing angrily. In the courtyard, I heard a centaur neigh. Why would they neigh when they had a human...? *Keep on track, Sarah.*

I cleared my throat. "Pixies? Ghosts? I know you're angry, but if you could all back off a bit and give Chip room to breathe, I'm sure he'll clear up this mystery for us in no time."

I raised an eyebrow his way. Chip slumped into his chair, rubbed his face, and sighed.

The pixies settled on the gleaming wood of the radio cabinet, and I felt the ghosts recede a couple of feet.

"You're right," he said. "I wanted a story. I know there's all sorts of activity going on behind the scenes in Seashell Cove. This place is a paranormal goldmine! I've seen proof! But no one in this town will even talk to me!"

"Could be because you're obnoxious," Stefon muttered. I elbowed his gut, which, as usual, was surprisingly hard.

"I saw the singer in the fossil store, talking with Tetris. They broke off when I walked in, but I heard enough." He looked in the general direction of the singer, but his eyes weren't fully focused, as if he could only see an impression of the two ghosts. "You weren't really here to record a new album. You wanted to sing in a haunted house, and see if the recording picked anything up."

Huh. Was this what Liam and Tetris were hiding? Were they in cahoots?

"Then what happened?" I asked.

Chip chewed on the edges of another fingernail. "I'd heard about the ghosts up here and broke in one night. The ghosts were excited. This one here said if only the singer would stay, her life would be complete."

He paused, licking at his pale pink lips.

"And?" Stefon asked.

"I had found a book, buried in the back of your store. I don't think you even knew about it."

"Wait a minute," I said. "You have never once purchased a book in my store!"

He shrugged and looked away again.

"You slimy little thief! You stole from me? And then accused me of murder?"

I shot out of my chair and towered over the cowering jerk, mad enough to spit.

Cyrus looked on, amused, but Stefon's hand landed on my shoulder. "Sarah."

I whirled, snarling in frustration. "He's a weasel, Stefon!"

"Now, now. Don't insult small animals. They all have a part to play in the ecosystem." Stefon smiled at me, with that look he gets that telegraphs just how much the big nerd loves and appreciates me. I couldn't help but smile back. A small one, but just enough to break the tension.

I shook out my hands and turned back to the so-called indie journalist slash paranormal investigator in his battered trench coat.

Which reminded me of Tetris. As soon as the thought flickered through my mind, the man himself burst into the room and leapt on Chip, pummeling him, spit and snot flying.

Well dang. Guess my psychic witchy powers are increasing.

"You killed her! You killed her! I heard you! Why? Why?" Each word from Tetris's mouth was coupled with a shove or punch. Chip grunted and cowered, trying to slap Tetris's hands away. The pixies returned to the fight, flying around both men's heads, tweaking Chip's hair and nose. The ghosts swirled, agitated.

"I didn't kill anyone!" he sputtered.

"Stefon?" I said, "you can step in anytime now."

He shrugged. "The man deserves to let off some steam, don't you think?" Arms crossed, he let Tetris get in a few more feeble smacks, then pulled him off. The metal staircase outside rang as if something hammered on the treads down below. Something...like an angry centaur's hooves.

Tetris bent over, hands braced on his knees, panting, his gray hair stuck to the sweat on his narrow face.

I'd truly had enough.

"All right," I said to the room. "Here's what's going to happen. We're taking this down to the dining room so the centaurs and Liam can hear what's going on, because I don't want to have to repeat this a million times. Ghosts? Come if you want, but don't throw anything. Pixies? Behave yourselves." And speaking of not repeating things...

"Uncle Cyrus? Can you get Cecilia, Toby, and the teens here, pronto?"

I wanted as many resources on hand as possible. I was going to figure out a punishment for Chip, and this tangled case had made it clear to me that I never knew who might have information I needed.

"We'll reconvene in fifteen minutes. Pixies, please tell the centaurs what's happening." They sped off without a challenge, thank goodness. And the ghosts began to filter from the room.

I approached the flapper, who glared at Chip as if she could kill him with her eyes. I didn't blame her one bit.

"You okay?"

Slowly, she turned her dark eyes my way, and smoothed a hand over her sleek bob, dislodging the fascinator once and for all. I reached to catch it before it fell to the floor. It slipped through my fingers anyway. Turns out that even though The Kelpie's ghosts can juggle physical objects, I have a long way to go before I can catch something from a ghost.

More to learn.

::Are you going to punish him?:: Her eyes were steady. Assessing me.

"As soon as we get the rest of the story out, I'll figure out a just sentence."

::Promise?::

"Promise."

What I didn't say was that I would mete out the best Justice I could. True justice wasn't always that easy to come by.

That fact became crystal clear when I saw the singer's face. She gazed at Tetris as if he was the moon and sun.

"Sharon?" he said. "Are you here?"

::I'm here, my love.::

My heart broke, then and there.

32

Once everyone was gathered, spilling into the kitchen and bar area, The Historic Kelpie's dining room was crowded. Too crowded. There were even ghosts hovering near the ceiling, and a few that simply poked their heads down from the second-floor parlor lounge.

Sometimes my life is seriously strange.

Most of the humans were gathered around the long, central table. Cecilia and Toby had arrived, as had Tabitha and Tracy, and Tracy's mother, Carol. Delta Crabbit sat next to me, with the gnome propped on a booster seat next to her. Stefon stood behind Chip's chair, which was just across from me, and Uncle Cyrus sat on my other side.

Liam sat at the head of the table in a weird, kitschy throne that looked as if it'd been liberated from some gothic castle. Sophie had arrived from somewhere, which was good. The housekeeper deserved to be a part of this, too.

The centaurs crowded just inside the doorway, lending a horsey smell to the proceedings, and the pixies perched on the back of the gnome's chair. For once, the art and bizarre mementos hanging all over weren't the weirdest things about the room, though I swore the mermaid winked at me from her painted rock.

What could've been a festive party had turned into a tribunal, mostly because Chip had decided not to talk.

"Isn't there some sort of magic lawyer to plead my case?" His voice had taken on a belligerent, whiny tone. I was seriously regretting not pumping him for more info when he was upset and confused up in the third-floor speakeasy.

"It doesn't work that way," I said.

"I still don't understand what happened," Liam said. He looked terrible, as if he hadn't slept in days. Sitting at his left, Tetris looked even worse, gaunt, as if he'd lost weight from his already thin frame.

I shoved my chair back and stood. If I was going to lay all of this out, I needed to pace. I made a shooing motion to the ghosts crowded closest to the table. They backed away, some of them joining the already packed booths that lined the walls. Ghosts didn't need to obey the laws of physics, did they? And apparently overlapping with your neighbor's shade wasn't a breach of ghostly protocol.

Good to know.

I cleared my throat.

"Here's the way I see it. Centaurs, pixies, and you two," I looked at the teens, who had books piled in front of them, "please chime in with any information you think I'm missing."

Toby and Cecilia walked around the table, pouring water for whatever humans wanted it. The hob just couldn't help themself. They had to either clean or make sure things were nice for everyone.

"Thanks, Toby." They blushed and nodded before moving on, finally taking a seat next to Cecilia once everyone was taken care of.

"Chip here needed a story. He was already onto the agreement you made with the pixies." I directed that toward the centaurs. Serafina simply tilted her head, waiting for me to continue. Fine. Play it that way. "You don't like to come to town, but there are certain herbs you need that don't grow deep in the forest, because there isn't enough sun. Right, pixies?"

Two of the pixies nodded, eyes large.

"You meet the centaurs in the garden here, to exchange the herbal concoctions for...?" That was one thing I hadn't figured out. What did the centaurs have that the pixies wanted?

"Tail hairs," the purple-winged pixie replied.

"Tail hairs?" Tabitha leaned forward, face alight with interest. "What do you use those for? Are they magic?"

"Of course, they're magic." Serafina snorted, tossing her head. "Everything about us is magic."

"We make jewelry out of them." The pixie with green wings touched a shimmering necklace that looked like a tiny, woven braid of black and silver.

"And beetle lassos."

"We haven't seen anything about that in the books

so far!" Tabitha said. Both teens bent their heads, Tabitha scratching in a notebook and Tracy furiously tapping away at her phone.

I didn't see evidence of that in the weird through-a-book realm I got sucked into, either.

"Beetle lassos?" Toby's head shot up, a beat late. "Doesn't that hurt them?"

"Of course not," purple wings said, her voice tinny with indignation. "But how else can we get them to pull things for us?"

Toby looked ready to retort, but I held up a hand. This was no time for an argument on pixie and beetle workplace politics. Besides, there was one other thing I needed to ask the pixies.

"Rowena? Do you know anything about spring being delayed?"

She cast her eyes down for a moment. "That is our way to mourn. We slow down the magic that helps things grow. Don't worry, things are speeding up again."

I looked at the teens, who were tapping into their phones. Good. That meant they were storing the new information.

But I still had too many questions, including the weirdness of the place with the ent named Uli.

I turned to the doorway. "Serafina? Is there something we need to know about the place..."

The black centaur snapped her teeth at me and held up a hand to stop the words forming in my mouth.

"You should never have gone there, and I will not speak its name. I can tell you that Uli is interested in meeting with you again someday, after the centaurs' names are cleared and some semblance of peace has returned to our realm."

Well, that was interesting, but didn't help much. The only thing it told me was that centaurs worked with tree-beings that were not dryads, and that pixies and centaurs—and beetles, apparently—had some sort of pact. There was way too much to learn about being a Justice.

"Okay, I'll have to trust your word and set that aside. For now." I paused, brain jumping through the facts as I saw them. "The white centaur—I'm sorry, I don't know your name."

"Máni," he replied. Huh. Like the Norse moon God. That fit his overall coloring, and his current disposition, which was decidedly remorseful and gloomy.

"Máni met the pixie to do the herb exchange. Chip told Sharon..."

I looked over to where the flapper and Sharon stood next to the centaurs and Tetris, arms around each other.

Two pixies burst through an open window, buzzing furiously.

"Lobelia! We figured it out! It was lobelia!" said one of the pixies.

"Tamina was always a glutton for it! She probably ate too much!" cried the other.

"Slow down!" shouted Rowena. "Where did the lobelia come from? This is not a plant we ever gather."

The beetle-green winged pixie looked at me and explained. "Lobelia causes euphoria in pixies when taken in small doses, but too much can be fatal."

And added to a potion that already contained digitalis and who knew what else? Could be fatal to a human with a weak heart, too.

"But where did the lobelia come from?" I asked. I had a vague memory of a bush like that in Toby and Cecilia's garden...

"From me," sobbed Tetris. "They were Sharon's favorite flowers. So small. Purple and pretty."

"Sharon? The one thing I can't figure out is why you drank the potion. And how the lobelia got into the vial."

She pointed to Chip. ::He told me it was magic, and that I needed magic to see and hear the ghosts better. And then the wee pixie told me that lobelia would heighten my psychic senses. I ate one flower before drinking from the vial. I must have dropped the rest of the flowers when I fell.::

Well, Chip and the pixie hadn't lied. It had all turned out to be tragically true. Sharon could see and hear ghosts just fine now. Because she was dead.

But what was I going to do about all of this?

"What happened to the rest of the lobelia?" I asked. "We didn't see it in the garden."

Máni hung his head. "I must have trampled them in my distress. I wasn't looking for clues, I just..."

So that explained the churned up earth I saw near the tree.

The two new pixies landed, one on each of his shoulders, stroking the centaur's long white hair as tears ran down his face.

"We finally found traces of it, buried an inch or two beneath the soil," said the pixie on Máni's right shoulder.

Sophie cleared her throat, which was a surprise. The housekeeper hadn't made a peep this whole time.

"Now that we've cleared up that mystery, I have something I need to say. You know. Before you sentence Chip, or whatever you're going to do." Every head swiveled her way. Sophie paused, looking slightly uncomfortable at the attention. "I think the ghosts want more respect. They complain about it all the time."

"They do?" Liam looked confused.

Sophie nodded. "People walk right through them, ignoring their existence. People abuse their nature, and their memories. They want someone to tell their stories, and to celebrate not just who they were, but who they are."

Well, and isn't that what every person wants? Is that what Biff wanted, too? I looked at Tabitha and Tracy, who nodded as if they'd heard my thoughts. Dang. Maybe I'd have to make Biff part of The Widening Gyre's advertising after all.

But first...

"Chip."

The reporter was covered in sick sweat and his swaggering bluster was gone. His eyes looked terrified.

"Did you know there were dangerous herbs in that vial? Like digitalis?"

"No! I didn't! I had no idea the singer had a weak heart! I never would have..." He burst into noisy sobs and cradled his face in his hands, shoulders shaking. I scanned his aura, seeking out any trace of dissembling.

"Cyrus?" I asked.

"He's telling the truth."

That made my job much easier.

I gathered my magic around me, and breathed in the authority that came with being Justice. Figuring out the crime had been a community effort, and Sophie's information about the ghosts let me know what a fitting punishment might be. It was less a punishment than it was recompense and accountability.

And I liked that.

"Chip Livingstone." My voice rang with all the power of my office. "I sentence you."

He cringed in his chair. Stefon laid a hand on Chip's shoulder, part to steady him, and part to keep him from bolting.

"Pixies?" I turned to the small beings clustered on the back of the gnome's chair. "Your fallen comrade was caught in the middle of Chip's machinations, though it was never his intention to harm your kind. Do you agree to abide by whatever sentence I issue?"

The smaller beings conferred for a moment.

"We agree," said green winged Rowena.

"You have done harm to the dead and the living of Seashell Cove. To pay back the community, I sentence you to live on the grounds of The Kelpie Inn and record the stories of all the ghosts here, and of any in town who wish to share their history with you, or to tell you about what their existence is like now."

I paused, and pointed to the flapper, who looked startled to be singled out. "Your part was unwitting, but you are to help Chip as an intermediary with the ghosts if he needs it. Do you agree?"

She nodded rapidly, then pulled out a snowy handkerchief to delicately blow her nose.

Note to self: ghosts still blow their noses. Seems

strange, but true. I turned back to Chip, who decidedly did *not* look like a man being sentenced for his crimes. Yet.

"Chip? After you interview the ghosts, you are to publish their stories in a series of volumes. The proceeds will go to Liam and The Kelpie Inn to pay for your room and board. Any money left over? Will benefit those beings in need in Seashell Cove, whether human or animal, magical or not."

A slow grin spread across the reporter's face. Well, I would stop that soon enough.

"And you will publish these stories under the name..."

I swear, every being in the crowded dining room leaned toward me.

"Anonymous."

Chip blanched, looking like he might throw up.

The rest of the room erupted in cheers.

33

"That was a pretty stringent sentence, Sarah," Uncle Cyrus commented. "Do you think it was fair?"

It was the day after the big events at The Historic Kelpie, and the centaurs and pixies had all returned to their homes. I'd invited whoever wanted to come to a small party in my backyard. That included Toby and Cecilia, who shared a bench together next to the arbor vitae hedge. Stefon sat next to me on another bench, opposite my best friend and her partner. The two teens and Tracy's mother, Carol, plus Delta Crabbit, Liam, and the gnome all sat in garden chairs I'd dragged out from the shed at the back of the garden.

We sat around drinking sparkling water and lemonade, enjoying the spring evening and my tiny slice of a backyard ocean view.

"Yeah," Tracy agreed. "Harsh."

I sipped at the lemonade and thought about it. "The

sentence had to be more than just a punishment. It had to be something that would somehow make amends—though what amends can actually be made when anyone dies? It made sense to use Chip's actual skills, but letting him publish under his own name would have given him what he wanted in the first place."

"It would have been a reward," Tabitha said, thoughtfully chewing on one of the shortbread biscuits Toby had baked that morning.

"Exactly," I replied. "Asking a writer to publish anonymously was the worst sentence I could think of that would still suit my purpose, which was to be of use to the affected community."

"I think it was just right," Delta chimed in, wiping crumbs from her face, then reaching for another biscuit, which she broke in half. One half went to the gnome. They were turning into quite good friends, those two. It was nice to see. Everyone needs a friend.

"Thanks, Delta."

Stefon squeezed my shoulder. "You did good, babe. But I hope you get a break now."

"Not if these two have anything to say about it." Carol smiled and poked her daughter's shoulder.

I groaned.

"We have a whole plan," Tabitha said, practically leaping from her chair. "We can bring it by the store after school later this week."

"Do I have to?"

"Do it for Biff, Sarah. It's what he wants." That was Tracy again. I looked at the blond teen more closely. Sure enough, she was serious. She knew something I didn't know. I looked at her mother. Carol smiled and nodded.

Huh. Tracy could speak to ghosts. Who knew?

I raised my glass of lemonade, and folks scrambled to refill empty cups and glasses until everyone had something to drink.

"I want to thank you all. We're becoming quite the magical community..." My throat threatened to close. Stefon squeezed my shoulder again.

"You got this, babe."

I inhaled. Exhaled. Felt the cool weight of the glass in my hand. Smelled the brine of the ocean and the warmth of my sweetheart at my side.

"We're becoming quite the magical community," I started again, "and it's something my parents would have appreciated, I think, if they'd only had the chance. They kept their support system pretty tight, as far as I know..."

Uncle Cyrus nodded.

"...but I think that this is better."

The threatening tears receded. Looked around the circle at these people whom I'd come to rely upon.

I raised my glass higher, the lemonade shining in the sun.

"To magic, community, and friends. And to working together."

"To working together!"

The toast rang through the garden. I kissed Stefon.

For the first time in a while, my heart felt light.

Things have gone missing in Seashell Cove, and more strange hijinks are afoot... Sarah, Rhiannon, and the gang are on the case! Read all about it in *Tarot Witch*.

ACKNOWLEDGMENTS

Thank you to Leslie and Jack for reading, to Dayle for editing, and to Robert and Jonathan for years of support.

And thank you to the 324 people who took a chance on my paranormal cozies for freaks and geeks. I'm speechless with gratitude for the Kickstarter support!

Most of you are listed below. For those anonymous ones who wanted no credit? Well, Rhiannon and Sarah know who you are.

A big, Kickstarter thank you to:

Abigail M. Fellnor, Adrian Emerson, Ahmarah, Aahzmandius, Alesia, Alexandra O'Bryan, Alison Naomi Holt, Allie Gentry, Alyson, Amara Snively, Ambar, Amy Montarbo, Andréa María, Angela Rain-catcher, Anna McCluskey, Anne E. Lynch, Annelise F.M., Annie Reed, Aramanth, Arianne, Becca, Becca K., Bonnie Elizabeth, Book Bunny, Breann Carpenter, Bookwyrmkim, Brad Snyder, Brendan "HollyKing" Leber, Brendon Reece, Bridgette Findley, Brooke Pratt, Carey Oxler, Carol, Carolyn Rowland, Carrie Boon, Cate Kneale, Catherine, Catriona, Céline Malgen, Bryn Hofmann, Celine, Charlie Boehme-Byrd, Chassidy

Strege, Cheryl Hammond, C. F Linnds, Chris Kaiser, Chris Paton, Christina Terhune, Cintia De Carvalho, CJ, Claire Manning, Claudia Nymphenkuss, CM Wolf, Colby Smith, Constance, Crystal, Dagmar Baumann, DL, Daniel J. Riddle, David H Hendrickson, Dawn McMorrow, Dayle Dermatis, Deanna Stanley, Debbie Mumford, Deb Bodeau, Deft, Della Keeley, Diana Deverell, Diane M Smith, Dianne M. Daniels, Diva Style Minister, E., E. Scott, E Dimopoulos, Efoy, Emily Pedersen, Emily, Emma Shelford, Enfys Book, Eric & Carla Chamberlin, Erin, Erin Ratelle, Erin, Faerie Sarah, Felicia Fredlund, Fennec Foxfire, Gemma, Georgette Paxton, Gertjan, GhostCat, Glenda Nowakowski, Goldie, Greenraven, Gwells, Hal, Hannah Golden, Heidi Moone, Helen Bridget Adeline Eastwood, Helen Hawk, Henry Espy Roberts, H Alexander Perez, Hobbit, Holly, Honoré Artaud, Imani J Dean, Inanna Hazel, Amy Laurens, Iris, Ivo Dominguez Jr, Izzy Hanelt, JK, Jim Gotaas, Jamie Forster, Janet Ní Shúilleabháin, Janette Fletcher, Janine Cobb, jaymi elford, Jeanna, Jeannine, JS Groves, Jenett, Jennifer Beltrame, Jennifer Bramhill, Jennifer, Jennifer Forness, Jennifer Mroz, Jessica F, Jessica Johansen, Jessica Marquardt, Jess Werner, Jinx, JoAnn, Johanna Rothman, John Bell, John Deltuvia, John W. Luther, Jon Auerbach, Jonathan Korman, Joe Cleary, Jaeelle Hayes, Julia Levine, Kajtryna, Karen Dougherty, Karen Snodgrass, Kat Humphries, Kate Pavelle, Kathryn F, Katina Clarke, Katy Manck – BooksYALove, Kaye & Sand, Kelly Chang, Ken Irwin, Kendall B, Kerry Paolucci, Kickstarter Music, Kim Z, Kirsten M. Corby, Kri O'Kellas, Kristen Gehrke, Kristin Rollins, Ladypants, Lanette

Miller, LaRena Rose, L. E. Knight, Leslie Claire Walker, Lezlie Revelle Zucker, Lilith, Liluri, Lily Wolthers, Lindsay DelGrosso, Lisa Costello, Lisa Sanger Blinn, Lora Shimer, Loren L Coleman, Lorelei Sherman, LaffingKat, Louisa Swann, Louise Lieb, Leigh Saunders, Mackensey S, Maddie, Maggie Fry, Mambo Chita Tann, Mar Azul, Margaret, Margit Hofmann, Marian Phillips, Marine Lesne, Marissa Schwartz, MoonCrone, Mark Carter, Mary Jo Rabe, MaryAnne, Matt Fabian, Maya Kate, Megan Potter, Merri Anne Stowe, M.G. Herron, Meyari McFarland, Michael Warren Lucas, Michelle Bryant Barbeau, Michelle Mishmash, Minkenstein, MJ Silversmith, Monica Van Steenberg, Morpheus Ravenna, Myke Johnson, Karen Fonville, name, Nancy Sloop, Nate Hernandez-Botma, Nathania Apple, Neil Coles, Niall Gordon, Nicole Lynch, Nicolina, Odd, Oliver Peltier, OwlLight, Phoebe Miller, pjk, Polly, POTU David, Author, Purple Steam Dragon, Quinn Kelly, R. Hunter, Rachel Peterson, Raven Cornelius, Rebecca Hiatt, Renee Rice, R.S. Kellogg, Rebecca M. Senese, Roxan, Richard A. Loftus, Richard Hoffman, River Roberts, Rob Vagle, Robin Hill, Rosalynde, Rrrose, Ru Temple, Ruth Wotton, Ryan M. Williams, Sage, Sage Cara, SallyRose Robinson, Samantha Landstrom, Sanchini Family, Sandra Choate, Sandra H, Sandra Mueller, Sanguine Kitty, Sara Blackthorne, Sara Ontiveros, Sarah, Sarah Underwood, Sarah A., Sarah Clark, Sea, Sea Queen, Shannon Davis, Sharon H, Sharon Rowse, Silke, Sioux Rowan, Skayle Bloodwomon, Sky Fowler, Simone P., Somcak, Sophia, souljacker85, Steph Wetch, Stephen VanWambeck, Stephanie Longoria, Stephen Ballentine, Steven

Whitacre, Steve Locke, Sunshine, Susanne Winter, Tasha Turner, Taylor Morich, Teri Moody, Thalassa, Thea Hutcheson, Thealandrah, Tina, T.L. Merrybard, Tony Malerich, Tony Rella, Tracy Eire, Two renegade Appalachians, Tyler Spencer, Visucien Fe, Valerie Herron, Valkyrie, Victoria S., Violet Twilight, Wendy Williamson, Will Gwaltney, Yuu Gamon

ALSO BY T. THORN COYLE

FICTION

The Panther Chronicles (Complete)

To Raise a Clenched Fist to the Sky

To Wrest Our Bodies From the Fire

To Drown This Fury in the Sea

To Stand With Power on This Ground

The Witches of Portland (complete)

By Earth

By Flame

By Wind

By Sea

By Moon

By Sun

By Dusk

By Dark

By Witch's Mark

The Steel Clan Saga

We Seek No Kings

We Heed No Laws

We Ride at Night

Seashell Cove Paranormal Mysteries

Bookshop Witch

Haunted Witch

Tarot Witch

Short Story Collections

A Hint of Faery

A Touch of Faery

A Spark of Magic

A Flame for Yuletide

A Hope for Winter

A Speculation of Stars

A Speculation of Hope

Risk It All: Queer Stories of Love, Suspense, And Daring

Thresholds: Queer Stories of Love, Suspense, And Daring

Non-Fiction

Evolutionary Witchcraft

Kissing the Limitless

Make Magic of Your Life

Sigil Magic for Writers, Artists & Other Creatives

Crafting a Daily Practice

ABOUT THE AUTHOR

T. Thorn Coyle worked in many strange and diverse occupations before settling in to write novels. Buy them a cup of tea and perhaps they'll tell you about it.

Author of the *Seashell Cove Paranormal Mystery* series, *The Steel Clan Saga*, *The Witches of Portland*, and *The Panther Chronicles*, Thorn's multiple non-fiction books include *Sigil Magic for Writers, Artists & Other Creatives*, and *Evolutionary Witchcraft*.

Thorn's work appears in many anthologies, magazines, and collections. They have taught magical practice in nine countries, on four continents, and in twenty-five states.

An interloper to the Pacific Northwest U.S., Thorn stalks city streets and talks to crows, squirrels, and trees.

Connect with Thorn:
www.thorncoyle.com

www.ingramcontent.com/pod-product-compliance
Lightning Source LLC
Chambersburg PA
CBHW071301190726
48292CB00007B/2639